CONFLUENCE

THE LIVING WORLD
BOOK THREE

CONFLUENCE

THE LIVING WORLD
BOOK THREE

Patricia Vestal

Sea of Mountains Press
North Carolina, US

Confluence: The Living World Book Three by Patricia Vestal

Paperback ISBN: 978-1-7375849-4-0

Published by Sea of Mountains Press, North Carolina, USA
www.seaofmountainspress.com

For permissions contact:
Website: seaofmountainspress.com
Email: author@seaofmountainspress.com

This is a work of fiction. Any resemblance to actual events or persons, living or dead, is entirely coincidental.

Cover and book design by: Michelle Triggs Owen, www.ProjectDesignInc.com

Cover image credit: NASA, ESA, N. Smith (University of California, Berkeley), and The Hubble Heritage Team (STScI/AURA)

DEDICATION

Dedicated to Frank and
those who cherish all living things

PROLOGUE

After eons of tranquil existence, the conscious energy that formed the Realm recognized that it was directly connected to another one of the universes that formed The Living World. Unlike the amorphous Realm, that universe had developed physicality. The Realm was directly tethered to one of the universe's planets that was evolving complex and diversified life. The Realm became aware that its purpose was to nourish and maintain this planet's connection to The Living World.

The Realm evolved in tandem with the planet, reaching out with tenacles of awareness through the Passageways that linked it to this new world. It developed into discrete energy-mind-spirit entities able to traverse the Passageways that deposited them on the material world, Earth. They came to call themselves Synons. They could think and act individually, just like biological life, but were intrinsically and eternally linked within the Realm and The Living World that encompassed all of Creation.

As Earth's life evolved through many ages, it reached the present one, in which humans had become the dominant species. Synons evolved with them as they visited Earth and used its ambient energy and matter to simulate individual life forms, particularly people. The Synons had to constantly learn, adapt, and build these complex personas, which included not only an individualized physical form but personality and behavior as well. Accessing human scientific knowledge, they had done this so well that tens of thousands of them now resided on Earth posing as people, the humans with whom they interacted never guessing they were not the of same species. Only a few people were capable of comprehending what the Synons were. Some had joined forces with them in what had become a mission to literally save Earth, the life she supported, the Realm, and The Living World.

CHAPTER ONE

The Realm shuddered, its tranquil, pastel energy glow flashing with deep reds and blacks. Synons, the energy-mind-spirit entities that formed that amorphous universe, strove to send calming energy through the Passageways tethering them to Earth. They were learning to manage the now frequent disruptions that zipped through Passageways as Earth's immune system reacted to what had become an invasive and destructive dominant species ravaging her domain.

On Earth catastrophe loomed.

■ ■ ■

Jeff Hawke sat in disbelief, head drooping. Around him, the other four human members of the Tech Team were just as stunned; the four Synon personas present projected apprehension. All sat silently around a table usually filled with cheer, in the gathering hall of their new summer camp nestled in North Carolina's mountains, to train telepaths they called Uniques.

Jeff managed to speak, but could only repeat what Bailey MacIntyre had just related. "So Mac, do I have this straight? You're saying that some far-fetched science fiction idea is real now? Earth is wobbling on her axis to a greater extent than ever before recorded? If her rotation rate becomes consistently erratic it could mean disaster? If she suddenly stops rotating, even for a second, everything could die immediately?" He exhaled loudly, raking a hand through dark hair as his eyes rose to meet those of the persona worn by his Synon friend.

Bailey MacIntyre's bushy brows furrowed as he answered. "Like with all potential phenomena, we have no actual evidence. Science has copious data on how our planet behaves. If there's an abrupt rotational halt, everything will be flung forward. Picture a fast-moving vehicle suddenly stopping. There will be devastating natural disasters like tsunamis, earthquakes, hurricane force winds. Natural and manmade objects of all sizes and weights will collide at high velocities. Living things will be caught in the crush, slamming against each other and objects.

We must urgently work to locate and prepare Uniques. Earth has already indicated to us that they might be the only hope for helping Earth control her responses."

■　　■　　■

The Realm reflected what was happening on Earth. The planet with which the Synons were intrinsically linked was becoming increasingly unstable as an ironic process unfolded. The humans they had guided for millennia were threatening to destroy the very planet that sustained them. Now Earth reacted violently, compounding natural disasters resulting from climate change primarily brought on by humanity. Earth appeared to be losing control of the complex systems on which survival depended.

Within the collective Synon minds, led by their strongest voice, TuMa'Aye Gra'Vay, a chorus rose. "As we are one, we send calming energy through every Passageway linking the Realm with Earth." A brilliant glow emanated throughout the Realm.

Another violent shudder threatened to rip it asunder. The Realm exhaled a collective sigh as it began gradually returning to its tranquil state, its glow once again a prism of gentle hues.

The entire globe dazzled as Earth was bombarded with lightning. As abruptly as it had occurred, it halted, followed by a multitude of rainbows. Momentarily, Earth was calm. Then the rainbows vanished and the instability returned.

■　　■　　■

In the past year, two people had demonstrated traits Synons had not seen in humans in recent history—Jeff Hawke and then five-year-old Emma Goodsen. They were dubbed "Uniques" by the Synons who were certain that others could be identified globally, but it would take time. The North Carolina camp was a prototype. Three children from the United States, including Emma, had been recruited to the new camp, while Synons living as people around the globe sought others.

The children were getting acquainted and oriented. They were glad to meet others like themselves.

They had just returned from a hike and were approaching the gathering hall for snacks. Through the windows they noticed the meeting in progress.

"Is it okay to go in there?" asked Tina. At nine, she was next to the youngest and a bit shy.

"Sure," Rick, the oldest at fifteen, asserted. "The canteen's right inside the door. We can be quiet and—"

Suddenly the chattering stopped. They looked at one another in astonishment.

Rick exclaimed, "Did you feel that?"

Eyes wide, Tina whispered, "Was it an earthquake?"

Although she was the smallest and youngest at six when they first met, the precocious Emma Goodsen's experiences of the prior year had made her the natural leader. To avoid having to look up at her companions as she spoke, she sat on the ground next to a tall oak. "I need a few minutes of silence," she instructed. The others nodded and sank to the ground, trying not to stare at Emma. "I'm closely linked to Jeff Hawke," she stated. "We only shield our minds from each other when engaged in personal thought and activity."

The other two children squirmed and looked pointedly at each other. Even though they had been identified as possessing the telepathic trait similar to Emma's, they were just beginning to comprehend what it all meant for them. Neither was able to perceive any mental energy from within the gathering hall where the Tech Team and Synons conferred.

Emma ignored their discomfort and continued talking. "Something very serious is happening with Earth. That's all I can make out. I'm getting disturbed energy from everybody in there. Open your minds and focus on them."

Rick challenged them. "Shouldn't we try to contact Earth to help?"

Tina looked at him with surprise, but Emma maintained control. "You've had almost no training. We have no idea what's wrong. And we should never go off on our own. The Synons have infinite wisdom. They've communed with Earth for ages. We need to wait for them."

Tina spoke up in a quiet voice, "I agree with Emma. We're novices. When the time is right they'll tell us what's going on and if there's anything they want us to do."

Rick leaned over and hugged the tree under which they sat. Eyes closed, he murmured. "Mother Earth, speak to us. Tell us how we can help you."

Emma chuckled. "You look like the cliché tree-hugger, Rick." The ice broken, the other two began laughing. Abruptly, silence fell and all, including Emma, wordlessly joined hands, eyes closed. After only moments, eyes popped open seeking those of their companions. Hands continued clinging to others.

"Such disorientation!" Exclaimed Rick. "Did everybody feel it?" Heads nodded.

Trembling, Emma murmured. "I felt like I was tilting in all directions, spinning fast, then slow. Something terrible is happening." She fell silent, turning toward the building. Jeff Hawke stood in an open window, glaring at them.

■　■　■

While the children were returning from their hike, those in the gathering hall sat in stunned silence.

"What do we do?" Jeff asked softly.

Mac sighed. "We don't yet know if this data portends dangerous events. For some time, the global scientific community will be diligently monitoring and reporting."

The children could hear the conversation in their minds. They looked at each other, trying not to laugh. "What's portend?" Rick sent his companions. They were becoming used to Mac's use of unfamiliar words in a way that Jeff humorously called "pedantic," which they didn't know either.

Of the other humans present, Chris Mills had become the most comfortable interacting with the Synons. He had been an integral part of their most recent mission, which had rescued young Emma Goodsen from an abductor. He spoke up. "Who do they report to?" He tugged at the long blond ponytail dangling across his shoulder.

MacIntyre responded quickly. "The United Nations. Even before this latest information, the UN had formed a task force on climate change to coordinate scientific data, recommendations, and action, in addition to ongoing disaster response. With geologists at the forefront, scientists are studying this new situation, correlating and analyzing data, and using AI and other technologies to model and predict the most efficient and effective actions that might be taken. Those most qualified will now focus on Earth's rotation."

Chris nodded. "So there's nothing specific we can do right now?" He looked disappointed.

Lewis Henderson interjected in his Appalachian Cherokee style of speech. "Seems to me that we need to keep working with these new kids. Just like Mac said, we have to get them ready quick if there's a chance they can soothe Mother Earth. People sure aren't doing it."

Jeff smiled behind the hand in which his face rested. He still marveled that Lew, his old friend, fellow Cherokee, and mentor, was actually an otherworldly being who, like Mac, had lived for decades on Earth in his current persona.

Henderson had barely uttered his opinion on the Uniques when Jeff and the Synons visibly reacted to some unseen phenomenon. The other four people looked questioningly at each other.

"What now?" Chris piped up.

None of those affected seemed aware of their companions or the question. Their eyes were glazed. Jeff sat stiffly, hands gripping the edge of the table. Then his eyes focused. He got up so quickly that his chair banged to the floor; he strode to the window.

The Synons looked like they were in a trance. The humans assumed they were talking to each other telepathically. As Chris again opened his mouth to speak, Jeff turned and almost ran out of the room toward the canteen.

The Synons returned to the moment.

Lew Henderson smiled. "Maybe I should have kept my mouth shut." He looked to the humans. "Did you feel anything at all?"

"No!" They all responded.

Lew nodded. "I thought so." He paused. "It seems our charges are ready to confront Earth. Or rather, they attempted it." Everyone waited for him to continue. He looked at Mac. "You want to tell them the rest?"

"No, you're doing fine." Mac chortled.

Lew described to them the sensations of disorientation and erratic movement they felt and had quickly discussed among themselves. "I think the kids and us Synons got a little dose of what Earth's experiencing. What we don't know is to what extent she can control it."

■   ■   ■

"What did you do?" Entering the canteen, Jeff approached the children, who wore sheepish expressions. They cowered at the volume and tone of his voice. He was always soft-spoken and gentle.

Emma stepped forward. "We felt her presence and just reached out instinctively. Then we felt her wobble. It was awful!" Her voice rose. "We have to help her!"

Jeff loudly exhaled in frustration. "You could have done something irreparable!" He sat in a chair glaring at them. His countenance and voice softened. "Look, I know you feel a strong purpose. So do I. Remember, I'm one of you. It's hard when we feel her. We just can't act impulsively. She's too fragile."

"There's something new with her, isn't there?" Emma stood before him as an equal.

He nodded. "We aren't sure about it. The scientists are trying to figure it out. Until they can give us some guidance we need to tread very softly."

"So can we stop playing camp and get to our training?" Emma demanded.

■   ■   ■

Bandela guffawed. Wearing the robes of his old archivist persona, he lounged in a Roman-style villa, constructed from a minute portion of the Realm's energy, engaging in his favorite pastime—observing human folly. Even though he had been sequestered within an inescapable force field in this tiny enclave of the Realm, his strength allowed him to read the thoughts of unsuspecting people on Earth. Synons were forbidden to invade the minds of others unless an immediate threat was posed, but Bandela disregarded it.

He especially enjoyed observing Roger Singleton, who had high brain function but was incredibly gullible. Greed and self-centeredness drove him, as it did most of his species. They ignored logical thought in pursuit of elusive delusions of wealth, power, and pleasure. Totally oblivious, they skittered on the edge of doom.

Bandela didn't realize that he lacked self-reflection as much as people did. His years of living among and emulating them had subsumed his innate Synon traits to the point that he had been willing to attempt the unspeakable—destroying his own kind.

The Synons were engrossed in efforts to save the world to which they were connected. They paid no attention to the only one of their kind whom they had ever seen the need to imprison.

Bandela was concerned that the Earth would become not only unlivable for biological creatures but useless for the technology-based entity that he planned to become to usurp human control.

CHAPTER TWO

"So what're these kids supposed to be learning?" Marie LaRue's eyebrows rose questioningly as she picked up her iced tea. She and the other team members had retired to the Tech Center deck overlooking the river, while Jeff and the Synons continued to confer. Mac had recruited the three members other than Jeff and Marie almost two years before, setting them up in this reclusive spot to facilitate the final steps of remotely reinstating the computer network Bandala had nearly destroyed in the Research Triangle city where Jeff and Marie had been colleagues and friends.

"Beats me," Mannie Patel shrugged, looking at Lana Adams. "Your voodoo senses telling you anything?" The two enjoyed a teasing, odd-couple friendship. He was an analytical New Yorker of Jewish and Indian descent; she had a background in psychology and cultural studies, flavored by her native South Carolina Low Country upbringing, with an African flair.

Lana threw him an exaggerated scowl, then her countenance turned serious. "Hopefully Earth will provide some guidance. The future of their generation is at stake."

Chris sniffed. "She hasn't so far. All she's put out is 'only they can help.' She hasn't said how." He looked at Marie. "You live with Jeff. Has he told you anything?"

She looked pained. "For most of the time we've been here he was forbidden to discuss with me any of his work with the Synons. I think he just got into the habit of…"

Chris looked embarrassed. "Sorry. Didn't mean to pry. I just thought since TuMa'Aye Gra'Vay, uh, Tami Graves said y'all were soulmates…." His voice trailed off just as Marie's had. Tami Graves was the persona of the Realm's most powerful Synon and an integral component of the upheaval that led Jeff and Marie to this place where they now shared a rustic cabin along a wooded creek with their companion cat Cosmos.

"It's okay, Chris. I've come to terms with the fact that although we really are soulmates, he's something I'm not. I've even got used to the telepathic conversations between him and Cosmos that exclude me." She smiled wistfully. "Of course, I love them both dearly."

Mannie was laughing. "So tell us how they talk to each other."

"They look at each other in silence. I can't explain it. Anyway, Jeff has major obligations now. I don't know where this will take him next."

Chris looked pensive. "He's the only adult Unique so far. Seems like they need many more if Earth thinks they can somehow persuade people to change their ways. It seems like for every two steps forward humanity takes, we go at least one step backward."

Lana spoke up. "Teens have been among the most effective leaders, in environmental and other issues. I don't think we should discount the power of young Uniques, especially if they can somehow link with Earth. Maybe they can give her the voice she doesn't have."

"Eloquently said." Mannie smiled.

■   ■   ■

The Synons decided to accelerate the training program. Mac was concerned about the gravity of ongoing scientific information he received. Earth's rotational fluctuations could be affected by events resulting from climate change and human activity, including techniques for extracting natural gas that could possibly be connected to earthquakes in places where they had never been experienced. Earthquakes often caused tsunamis that were becoming more frequent, especially in the Pacific. Earth was under extreme duress.

There were only two long-term Earth-dwelling Synons at the camp: MacIntyre and Lewis Henderson. The other two, Annilu and Judilay, were still learning how to interact with humans but had been selected for their telepathic strength. The two "newbies"—as Jeff called them when he had been charged with shepherding their initial foray into human society—were excited about the camp and wanted to be involved in working with the kids. Judilay, especially, was developing an affection for people. He hoped to be able to travel to other countries as a camp emissary. Annilu was more aloof, with an academic attitude toward Synon-human interactions.

The training began with exercises in the trait setting Uniques apart: telepathy. The kids were relieved to acknowledge this ability, after having concealed it in their daily lives, even from their families. It was refreshing and liberating to openly discuss it. They seriously applied themselves to the exercises, which at first were exhilarating. They practiced encounters face-to-face, apart, and in groups with Jeff, and Synons, gradually at increasing distances. Telepathy was so innate to Synons that it was difficult for them to understand how much energy it took for humans. The children tired quickly.

Jeff and Emma urged patience on the Synons. Their own discoveries of this ability had been accidental—Jeff's by joking to his Synon friends about communicating with his cat, which controlled experiments verified. He had not allowed himself to acknowledge the small incidents when he was growing up in Cherokee, steeped in traditional Native American and contemporary culture. Emma was younger, and, like many children, loved imaginary worlds and creatures. She accepted that fairies were real and was not shocked when she had been visited by one. She now knew that fairy had been Annilu desperately seeking a viable Passageway in the midst of cascading natural disasters.

The prior year Jeff and Emma had been forced to acknowledge their abilities when she and Jeff had inadvertently telepathed with each other. Jeff was working undercover as a security guard using the name Jeff McCarthy at the mansion of Roger Singleton, who was suspected of holding the abducted Emma. Jeff had been stunned by the sudden sound of a child's voice in his head asking if he was a fairy. He stood on the patio and she sat imprisoned on the second floor. This encounter led to her rescue and a special bond between them.

Emma and Jeff were empathetic and caring in their work with the children, referring to their own experiences and feelings as they had learned to cope with being Unique. The Synons saw that they needed to train these few to become trainers.

■　■　■

Emma sat on the grass, shaking, eyes glazed. "Are you okay, Emma?" Joy chased concern across Jeff Hawke's face. She nodded.

Jeff sat next to her, encircling her shoulders with his arm. "I'm so proud of you." A smirking grin claimed his face. "And you stole my record as the only known human to go through Passageways." His grin widened.

"You're the first man. I'm the first girl." Emma grinned up at Jeff.

"The first of what we hope will eventually be many." Lewis Henderson's lanky, aged, persona sank down on the other side of Emma.

In addition to linking the Realm to Earth, Passageways on Earth provided quick transit for Synons from one spot to another. Now two humans had been guided on short trips through them in what the Synons predicted would become a precedent for other Uniques like Jeff and Emma. However, the other children were cautious about trying to go through Passageways. They still grappled with the existence of things that seemed to be too much like the popular culture depictions of black holes. Neither volunteered to be the next Unique to try traversing one.

The other Synons gathered around Emma. Judilay whooped, his long black dreadlocks bouncing in the air. Annilu gave him a stern look. "The occasion calls for a little more dignity," she proclaimed, tapping the toe of a gleaming white sneaker under her pressed khaki slacks. These two had reason to celebrate; they had facilitated Jeff's safe and successful travel from one Passageway to another and now repeated the process with Emma.

Bailey MacIntyre stood to the side, the breeze blowing his shoulder-length gray hair. His lined face beamed as he surveyed the scene. His eyes swept beyond the shaded clearing among old growth trees to the wide area that now sprouted varied-sized cabins encircling a pond. Narrow gravel roads snaked among flowers, bushes, and trees. Through the woods was the old farmhouse where he and Lew lived, hosting visiting Synons. In the other direction was the refurbished motel that housed the single tech crew members, not far from Jeff and Marie's creek-side cabin. He was pleased.

■　■　■

"We need to contact TuMa'Aye." Mac motioned to Annilu and Judilay. "You two come with us to form a link to the Realm." He stalked out of the building, followed by the other three Synons.

Emma and the group of adults left looked at one another knowingly. The new children looked confused and amazed. "Who is Two...what'd he say?" Rick asked.

The adults laughed. Jeff answered. "TuMa'Aye. Sounds like," he proceeded to pronounce the name phonetically. "Two, Ma, like in Mama, and A like the letter A as in May. TuMa'Aye. That's just the first part of the name. The next part is like our last names. Grah, it rhymes with Aah." He opened his mouth wide, "Vay, rhymes with say." He said the entire name again. "TuMa'Aye Gra'vay. Her persona has an easier name, Tami Graves."

The new children sat with mouths open. Rick appeared to be the only one capable of speaking. "And she's in the Realm now?"

"I think so." Jeff said with a grin.

"And these Synons here are going to talk to her?"

"Yep. That's how powerful Synons are."

■　■　■

The four Synons melted into the forest, changing to their natural formless states of energy. They hovered over a babbling stream, light encircling them. Even though Mac and Lew were each capable of telepathing with the Realm solo, it would be good practice for Annilu and Judilay. They directed energy and thought through the Passageway embedded in the stream, facilitating a quick link to the Realm that was immediately severed. When they repeated the attempt, the four on Earth were suddenly buffeted by their own energy catapulting back onto them. They separated, retreating to the forest in efforts to maintain the integrity of their essence.

The Realm was under assault from Earth. Barrages of power spewed from more Passageways than they had thought still existed. Their entire universe swirled with cyclones of force that collided with its ambient energy, emitting sparks and shafts of lightning, its tranquil, pastel hues now streaked with bold black and red.

TuMa'Aye Gra'Vay tried to calm the Synon turmoil, but her thoughts merely dissipated. If this continued the Realm could be torn asunder. TuMa'Aye abruptly recalled the cyberspace attacks she had experienced from Bandela on Earth. She managed to link with Tork, who was second only to her in strength. "Where is Bandela?" she asked.

Tork struggled to move closer to her. "He's within his prison. I hope it can hold up against this." Both reached out but were unable to locate Bandela's signature.

CHAPTER THREE

As she had promised, once Bandela was safely contained in the Realm, TuMa'Aye Gra'Vay had revisited what her Tami Graves persona regarded as a clever play on words—the biker-bunnies.

It was easy to locate the eight rabbits in the wooded area where she and MacIntyre had left the renegade Synons. Tami had tried to infiltrate their group as a new persona, but its leader, Bret, immediately recognized her mental signature in spite of her potent barrier. Tami had been alarmed at the degree of evolution their human personas displayed and used in ways that conflicted with the Synons's nature and missions.

She and MacIntyre had followed them one night as they drove into the country on their motorcycles. They were discovered in their natural form stealing power from an electric substation then attempting to destroy a Passageway in the adjacent forest. Weakened by their efforts, the eight had been mere blobs of energy with barely enough strength to beg not to be sent back to the Realm. They pleaded that they had been on Earth too long living as people and couldn't readjust to their universe of origin. Tami had compromised by turning them into rabbits to live where they were while she discussed them with the Realm. It would take the entities that formed the rabbits some time to regain enough power to rebuild their human personas. Meantime, Tami ordered the area predators not to hunt them. The extensive data she had ingested from her recent forays into the internet had swiftly provided not only rabbit anatomy, but survival instructions for them as well.

Once Bandela was sequestered in the Realm she approached the rabbits as Tami Graves, knowing they would recognize her Synon identity. They had stayed close together, sharing the knowledge that always seemed to pop into their minds when needed for survival.

She sat on the ground looking at them. "I can't let you go back to your human personas."

Bret screwed up his face, nose twitching. His deep human voice sounded hollow in her mind. "Please! We can't endure the winter out here."

"I don't know if you can be trusted not to stir up trouble again."

Contrite, they all protested at once, bombarding her mind with pleas.

The core Synon nature harbored no malice. Those in the Realm had been flabbergasted and horrified at the behavior of the Synon renegades recently discovered on Earth; they reflected the worst of human nature.

Tami pondered a few minutes, then proclaimed, "Stay close to this spot. People will come with animal crates and take you to a shelter where you'll be cared for in safety until we decide what to do with you."

"Crates? You mean cages?" Bret squeaked.

One of the other rabbits summoned the courage to speak. "Will it be real people or personas?"

"Strong Synon personas."

"How long will it be?" Bret's tone was demanding.

"A few days. As I said, hang around here. I'll give a new warning to predators as I'm leaving."

She rose and glided away as the biker-bunnies scampered to cover.

■　　■　　■

The rabbits were taken to a shelter for injured or mistreated animals and placed in an enclosure. The caretakers talked to them, sometimes in human language, and at other times telepathically. The bunnies assumed this was to intimidate them with reminders of their overseers' power. They withstood a long winter, glad to be warm and well fed.

As their strength gradually returned, the rabbits pretended to still be weak, although they feared the caretakers would sense their growing power. Once spring arrived they felt compelled to escape. They had been told about Bandela's fate. They would not be taken from this animal cage to a forcefield cage in the Realm.

The Synon caretakers had some difficulty communicating with actual wild animals whose minds differed from creatures that had long been domesticated and lived among people. The animals sensed that those who fed them were kindred spirits, but their self-preservation instincts incited distrust.

Two mountain lions had arrived as cubs. Their mother had been shot as she defended her den from humans. The cubs would have perished if not found and brought there. Now they had grown into their full size and strength. They were within a sizable habitat but had discovered its perimeters that were surrounded by high fencing; nightly charges and attempts to jump over it became a favorite pastime. One evening a fierce thunderstorm produced a lightning bolt that struck a tree next to the fence. Fire ensued, jumping the fence. Like all animals, the lions had an inborn fear of fire, but they saw that the barrier beyond the flames was being pulled down as the fire destroyed an attached fence portion. They swiftly took advantage of the opening only to find themselves tumbling into a river that they were forced to swim. On the other side of the river they found another high fence but were able to scale it to complete their escape.

Visible, but not comprehended by the mountain lions, were cameras providing the caretakers with full views of the enclosure. The fire and subsequent escape were immediately seen, setting into motion a contingency plan. The mountain lions could not be allowed to roam in the surrounding wildlife refuge. In addition, they had grown up in captivity and were not equipped to survive. Their adventure ended before dawn when they were recaptured and secured.

The daily routine included ensuring that all compound inhabitants were fed and in good condition before night fell. Even though some of the animals were nocturnal, many slept, aware that they were safe. As this night came alive with lights, noise and activity, no one was concerned with the rabbit enclosure once it had been checked. The bunnies saw their own chance for escape. They easily threw off the rabbit personas, and in their natural forms left the enclosure and the compound. Under the cover of night, they reached out to kindred renegades who guided them to their location. Time to get back to work.

■　　■　　■

TuMa'Aye Gra'Vay had been absorbed in establishing communication and cooperation among the multitude of Earth-dwelling Synons living in small groups. Many had heeded her call for aid in battling Bandela and his renegades when he had invaded and was destroying a municipal cyber system with the objective of expanding his control. She had been stunned at the number of Earth-Synons discovered locally and globally. Now processes were being established for effectively locating and recruiting Unique humans. She had allowed her priorities to focus too sharply, losing sight of the threats from their own. Despite the many cooperative Earth-Synons, renegades were still operating in opposition to the Realm.

The assault on the Realm abruptly ceased, and circumstances gradually returned to normal. After an extensive search, no sign of Bandela was found. Locating one Synon on the planet could be next to impossible. He could be anywhere, employing effective shielding to prevent other Synons from locating him. TuMa'Aye Gra'Vay was determined not to allow him to create more havoc. She decided to go to Earth herself to oversee the search.

The former biker-bunnies encircled Bandela, keeping an awed distance. They were exhausted and weakened. The personas of some flickered. Pride in their accomplishment sucked in ambient energy, replenishing them. Bandela was also spent, struggling to maintain his old Dr. Gabe Jackson persona while establishing control over these Earth-Synons. They were a small number of those around the globe who had synchronized an attack on the Realm strong enough to allow these few here to strengthen a Passageway and aid Bandela in using it to pass from the Realm to this spot.

Bandela concluded that a little praise would be helpful. "Well done!" His arms were swept out in a symbolic gesture of embrace. "When we've all recovered our strength, we must establish a global connection expressing our esteem for those who joined this effort. This is the first step in a plan that will ensure our dominance of this planet!" He was experiencing the same problem maintaining his persona as when he had previously incarnated the biomechanics scientist Jackson. This time, he was sure that it was simply depleted strength. He wouldn't allow it to be an impediment. "We all need rest. Where is the place you have for me to retire?"

A young woman spoke deferentially. "Sir, follow me. We hope this will suffice. It was difficult to find an available and secluded home befitting your stature."

He nodded. "I appreciate your consideration and efforts. I'm sure it will suffice for a short time. Lead on." As he stepped forward, the Earth seemed to tilt beneath him. This was something new. Within the group he sensed concern.

"Sir, did you feel that?" the young woman inquired.

"I did. What was it?" Jackson was relieved. It wasn't connected to his fluttering persona.

Bret replied. "We're aware of frequent fluctuations in the planet's rotation. We can't ascertain its cause."

"Are the Earthlings aware of it?" Jackson snapped.

"We here don't know. Renegades within the sciences might."

"I have a contact for you to locate as soon as you've rested. Now let's go." As they started walking away, he felt another, sharper, movement as if the ground were rocking.

CHAPTER FOUR

Roger Singleton grabbed his brandy and stalked onto the balcony. The cool breeze wafting off the Gulf of Mexico should have calmed him, but he was in a fury. For over a year, he had struggled not to ruminate on lost opportunities and near personal disaster, forcing himself to focus on his robotics business. Now he couldn't stop the rush of frustrated anger. He had almost thrown a chair at his huge television when Suki Kurosawa suddenly appeared on it.

It hadn't taken long for Roger Singleton's staff to ascertain that the woman calling herself Kim Sawa was actually a reporter named Suki Kurosawa. By that time, however, they were unable to locate her. Nor could they find Jeff McCarthy, who had whisked her away from Singleton's charity party where she obviously had been snooping. Then after mustering out from his gig as a guard for the party, McCarthy turned out to be conspiring with the very aliens to whom Singleton sought to offer his services. The aliens disappeared along with McCarthy. Singleton fumed. He had placed himself in jeopardy to kidnap the brat, Emma Goodsen, aiming to force her to lead him to her alien friends. Now she was under tight security. Her family had changed and secured their contact data. They had enrolled her in a guarded private school. Now his sources reported the Goodsens had recently vacationed in the North Carolina mountains and returned home without the girl. Singleton was smart enough not to make another move on her. Could this Kurosawa be of help?

Everybody had disappeared! He couldn't even locate the famous biomechanics roboticist, Dr. Gabe Jackson, to offer him a partnership deal. He figured this Jackson was working with extraterrestrials. How else could he have made such progress? The aliens had to be causing all this climate mayhem. What was their game?

Singleton thought back over the events leading up to his encounter with them and their sentient craft. There had been vivid sightings around the time that a freak hurricane veered from the Gulf south of Naples, Florida straight into the Everglades. It had been a small, compact storm that left so little damage to the surrounding area that Singleton had not had to cancel a large gathering at his coastal home shortly after the storm moved through the center of Florida and into the Appalachians. The hurricane had confounded meteorologists. Singleton wondered if the aliens somehow affected or directed that storm? If so, for what purpose?

Word among his sources was that the Earth's axis rotation was becoming increasingly erratic. Were the aliens behind that? How could he ally with them? If they were planning on destroying the planet, he needed to think beyond immediate profit and power to his own survival.

■   ■   ■

"Mr. Singleton, Dr. Gabe Jackson here. I understand you wanted to talk to me." Bandela shrewdly turned around his own desire to learn what Singleton might know by replying to an old message from Singleton to his Jackson persona, proposing they discuss working together.

Roger Singleton was taken aback. "Uh, oh, yes. Yes! Thank you for calling."

"Well, Mr. Singleton, I looked into your work and am impressed at your robotics accomplishments."

"Thank you!" It was unlike Singleton to gush, but he was thrilled to hear from Jackson. "Your biomechanics work surpasses mine. I'm so excited to talk to you." Control returned as his mind, coiled around his ambitions. "We appear to excel in different areas of the same general field. I think we could go into lucrative new territory as partners."

Jackson changed the subject. "By the way, before our conversation continues, I must remind you that I am still in seclusion. I want no word to leak out that I've contacted you. To be blunt, only a few staff know my whereabouts and I must keep it that way."

"I fully understand. You can rely on my silence. However, is it possible for us to meet to discuss my ideas? You're welcome here, of course. My staff is carefully curated and trained."

"First, I need to know what it is you propose? I might have absolutely no interest."

Singleton knew he had to hook Jackson quickly. "You've done superb work in prosthetic limbs that connect to the wearer's brain. I'm working on artificial intelligence far beyond anything I've patented or made public. Together, we could build a prototype android."

Jackson mused, "I'm intrigued. By the way, I've heard some tantalizing rumors about the Earth's rotation becoming irregular. Can you point me to anyone working on that?"

Singleton knew he could locate someone through his labyrinth of contacts, so was confident in his reply. "Of course. I've seen some reports on this. Quite extraordinary. I'll have someone get in touch with you. Can I give them this number?"

"Yes. I appreciate that. I'll be in touch again soon." The call ended.

Stunned, Singleton sat a moment then called his assistant to begin preparations for a distinguished visitor traveling incognito.

◼   ◼   ◼

Bandela smirked, tweaking his Gabe Jackson persona of an aging, slightly paunchy man with balding white hair. This Singleton had appeared to be a fool, attempting to cultivate Synons posing as covert extraterrestrial invaders. However, his public work hinted at some degree of knowledge and talent. If he by any chance had made progress in constructing androids, he could be useful. Bandela had no interest in artificial intelligence. He wanted a simple, durable body in which to encase his essence. Once he had that he could explore future options and opportunities. The entire human race had not evolved efficiently. They could be easily manipulated and dominated.

He would spend a minimum amount of time ascertaining any value Singleton might offer.

◼   ◼   ◼

Within a few days of his conversation with Singleton, Bandela-Jackson was surprised to get a call from a planetary scientist who said he was calling as a professional courtesy in light of Dr. Jackson's reputation; however, he could offer no concrete answers. "As of now, there is no cause for concern. The fluctuations are within normal potential deviations."

"I'm curious as to what could be the cause," Jackson replied.

"Numerous factors such as seismic activity, or even a natural extraction technique called fracking. We're looking into any possible impacts of severe climate events and melting glaciers. So far, as I said, these erratic movements are so insignificant as to not raise the slightest hint of alarm. Of greater concern is the rising incidence of earthquakes and tsunamis."

"Well, that's a relief, at least regarding the rotational issue. It does appear that rumors are beginning to circulate."

"That's unfortunate, especially if it seeps into the media. The public seems so prone to concoct and disseminate outlandish stories from the slightest thread of misinformation."

"Quite so. Before we know it, they will be proclaiming that extraterrestrials are controlling the planet." Jackson barked a laugh. "Please do notify me if the situation changes. I'm on a secluded sabbatical right now but can use my considerable influence if necessary and advisable."

The call concluded with a few more pleasantries. Bandela was finding it easier to occupy his Jackson persona and interact as the renowned scientist he had been. He could use Dr. Gabe Jackson to his advantage. He had to practice *being* the person.

CHAPTER FIVE

People went about their daily routines blissfully ignorant of the ominous new threat. Many continued to deny that the now consistently tumultuous climate was the result of human activity causing the planet to warm. They tended to think about it only when experiencing severe weather or geological events, despite frequent warnings from scientists, government officials, and the media.

■   ■   ■

On Japan's eastern coast, Your Cable News reporter Suki Kurosawa was about to wrap up the story of its traditional fishing communities. She peered out to sea as gusty wind threatened to topple her into the roiling water below.

"Suki! Get back! You're way too close to the pier's edge!" Stan, her exasperated producer, moved as if about to yank her away.

Suki waved him off, speaking as she moved back a few feet. "I want shots of this churning water. It's lapping almost to the top of the dock. And then a long shot out to sea. Look how dark it is. The clouds seem to be touching the water at the horizon."

Stan motioned for their small crew to set up. "I don't like the look of it," he said. "We need to shoot and wrap up fast."

"No live feed?" Suki looked disappointed.

Stan laughed. "Jet lag's really got you. It's about three a.m. in New York. Live report would be wasted." He looked behind him. "We could start with the establishing drone shot of the village we did earlier to show how close the people live to the water. We can overlay your narrative in editing."

"Okay. I like that." Suki agreed.

As Suki began turning so that the sea would be behind her for the shot, the cameraman, who was looking through his telephoto lens, shouted. "Giant wave! Everybody run!" He started running backward, shooting as he went.

    ■   ■   ■

"We're sorry to wake you so early, Ms. Schechner."

"What's happening?" Vera Schechner, News Director of Your Cable News, demanded, as she scrambled out of bed. The graveyard shift wouldn't be calling at that hour unless it were of utmost importance.

"Sending you raw footage from Japan."

"Kurosawa?" At Suki's request to do a human-interest story, Vera had sent the Japanese American reporter to the home village of her uncle, who had been lost with other fishermen to a freak tsunami the prior year.

"We've lost touch. But," he hastily added, "they were able to upload this footage. We need to know if we should run it."

As he spoke, Vera booted up her laptop and opened her secure link to a jumble of voices accompanied by a flurry of jerky, unfocused images of a wooden dock receding, revealing an ominously black sky touching what looked like a dark, high wall. The camera revolved to show a vehicle. More images and sounds lasted only a few seconds until the feed suddenly cut off.

Vera touched the phone lying next to the computer. "Did you have any direct contact?"

"No."

"See if the techs can get any more out of this. Do not share it with anybody else."

*   *   *

Within the chaos Suki heard the sound of an approaching helicopter. The noise increased as the wind picked up all around them. The SUV into which she and the crew had scrambled jerked violently. She shrieked as she felt herself being lifted off the ground.

"Keep the windows up!" Stan shouted. "Buckle in! I went through this in the military."

Suki was able to maintain her equilibrium to peer out the closed window. They were flying! Above their vehicle loomed a helicopter towing them low enough for protection against the whirling blades but higher than the village structures. In minutes they approached the inland hills and were being gently lowered to the ground.

"Stay still 'til they have us untethered and the chopper has lifted off," Stan ordered.

A ground crew appeared, stooping over to avoid the blades and the wind gusts they created. Suki felt the vehicle being disconnected. The chopper's noise receded as it lifted off. A face appeared outside the window motioning her to open the door to the rear passenger compartment where she crouched.

The cameraman, sitting in the SUV driver's seat said in a shaky voice, "I just unlocked the doors. It's safe to get out."

Suki fumbled to unhook the seatbelt and reached for the door handle. As she bent over, a wave of dizziness hit her, and she almost fell. The man outside opened the door and grabbed her.

"You're okay," he assured her. "Don't stand until you feel steady."

She slowly slid out of the vehicle and stood leaning against the SUV, taking large gulps of air, fighting down nausea.

"Hold on," the man muttered, holding her arm. "Brace yourself until that chopper lands." She realized that another large helicopter was landing nearby. She tried to look around and get her bearings. Stan and the other two members of her crew also were braced against their vehicle, looking curiously around. The cameraman opened the passenger side door and grabbed the camera from the floor. He adjusted it and began shooting.

Suki saw that they were in a rescue staging area. It looked like a plateau atop a hill or low mountain. What was obviously a makeshift helicopter landing area was roped off. Beyond, she saw cars, trucks and buses parked, while more arrived from a road that obviously wound upward from the village area. In another section large tents were being erected with people being directed toward them. The people bore bundles of clothing, handbags and tote bags, briefcases, varied types of sacks, plastic garbage bags, and pet carriers. Some held cats and small dogs tightly in their arms or led dogs on leashes. A sense of relief and gratitude, tinged with sadness washed over Suki.

"We'll help you gather your belongings from this vehicle and get you settled," the man who had helped her was now talking to Stan. "Do you mind if we use it for additional rescues?"

"I suppose so," Stan mumbled. "It's rented." He chuckled. "This will be some expense report to hand in to YCN. Better get Vera on the phone asap."

Suki was taken to a tent filled with women and small children and shown to a cot among many lined up like a barracks. Even though she was of Japanese descent, she felt awkward among these natives who chattered quietly as they arranged the meager belongings they had been able to grab. Children cried. Several villages were represented, so they weren't all acquainted, but it seemed everyone knew someone who knew someone else. Greetings and introductions were accompanied by grasped hands and a few hugs. No one seemed to notice her.

Exhausted, she gratefully lay back on the cot assigned to her. Fatigue claimed her; she surrendered to sleep.

■   ■   ■

Huddled in their hilltop tents, the refugees were too far away to see what happened to their picturesque villages dotting the narrow strip of land along the shore. No one was present to record the wall of water rising up to devour the wooden structures covered by colorful tile roofs, many with multiple stories fronted by porches. Like toys menaced by an angry child, they were swept from foundations, splintered and crushed. Graceful trees snapped, joining the flotsam of people's lives mangled and washed from homes and businesses to rush along the streets that had become raging rivers. Manicured flower and vegetable gardens drowned in salt water. Stray and wild animals struggled in terror only to succumb to the overwhelming crush of water.

■   ■   ■

Suki wanted her viewers to experience what it was like for people to unexpectedly lose loved ones to a natural disaster. She wanted apathetic viewers to feel the grief. She wanted to wake them up to what was happening around the world. To make them do something. Her story had been planned to be about the loss of village fishermen, now it would show the survivors of these villages who had lost everything. Everything but their lives; gratitude would be touched by grief for those unable to escape, for the loss of homes and possessions, cherished family keepsakes, livelihoods, memories of the place that had been an anchor of comfort and security.

She would tell their story.

■　■　■

Suki and the crew relocated to a more inland village that had taken little damage. From there they could return to the relocation camp and the coastal villages to continue reporting.

As she was gathering her things to depart, Suki tried to avoid an older Japanese woman named Akari who was the only person to befriend her there, but she always seemed to be hovering around, asking questions. Now Akari saw Suki packing and rushed over, "Oh, no! Are you leaving?"

Suki didn't make eye contact, continuing her packing. "Yes. YCN is moving us."

"Moving you? Out of Japan?"

Suki hesitated, knowing Akari would easily see her interviewing the displaced villagers. I'm not sure." She slung her duffle onto its wheels and hefted her backpack. "Best to you," she said, hurriedly turning her back and moving away.

■　■　■

Everyone at the camp lounged in the gathering hall after dinner. Now, they watched one of Suki Kurosawa's reports on the Tsunami aftermath. A drone's camera feed glided over the rubble of what had been villages, Suki's voice narrating. She related how suddenly the wall of water appeared and the quick warnings of watchers that initiated the implementation of evacuation plans.

There were shots of the evacuation camp where everyone seemed busy with a task, including Suki who was serving food to a line of people. As the camera moved among the people, Mac suddenly exclaimed, "Go back. Freeze that shot."

Chris picked up the remote and complied. "Here?"

Mac nodded, getting up and walking to peer at the screen. "Lew, look at this older woman standing next to Suki. Have you seen her before?"

Lew joined him, examining the image of the woman. "Something about her...I'm not sure." He shook his head.

■　　■　　■

After they were relocated and YCN began showing her segments, Suki was surprised to get a text from Bailey MacIntyre. It merely read: "Older Japanese woman serving food next to you might be a spy. Keep away. Delete these texts and this number."

He had to be referring to Akari. The woman seemed to know too much and asked too many questions. Also, Suki had noticed that she had few acquaintances among the locals.

But why was she prying into her life? Suki's skin crawled, recalling her first communication with MacIntyre: a terse phone call warning that Singleton had sent dangerous people after her. His agent, Cal Booker, had whisked her away from her New York apartment to a safe house. She had never returned to her cozy home. Her furniture had been placed in storage; she had moved among short-term rentals ever since.

She had been foolish to think she could manipulate a man like Roger Singleton in her quest to find out if Emma Goodsen was imprisoned in the living quarters that were off-limits to guests at the lavish party she had attended as Kim Sawa. She had been lucky to escape unharmed. Apparently, Singleton saw her as a loose thread, or someone with connections he wanted to follow. His motives were murky but intimidating. The fact that he might have actually sent an operative to find her in Japan was terrifying.

CHAPTER SIX

MacIntyre was surprised to hear the voice of TuMa'Aye Gra'Vay in his mind. "May I visit the Tech Center?"

"Are you in the Realm?"

"Yes. I have urgent business on Earth and need a base."

"Of course. It's a relief to hear from you. We couldn't communicate with the Realm."

"We were attacked. Can I come now?"

"We have several human Uniques here. They know what we are, but have only interacted with us when we appear human. You need to show up in a normal manner as Tami Graves."

"Is anyone who knows me away from the compound right now?"

"Yes. Marie's in Asheville shopping."

"I'd enjoy a little away time with Marie. Show me her location."

Mac's mind roamed; it found Marie loading the back of her vehicle outside a health foods market. Mac shared the location with TuMa'Aye. "She's in a busy location, unfortunately, but it's not far from the river. You can probably find a Passageway along the banks there, although people could be nearby."

"I've got it. I've transformed in some unlikely places, believe me."

Mac chuckled as the Tami Graves persona's wry humor emerged. "I'll call Marie and tell her to stay in the parking lot and watch for you."

"Thanks. I've found a suitable Passageway. Get on the phone."

■　　■　　■

"What? How's she gonna get here from the river?" Mac had caught Marie just as she was buckling up for the drive home. "It's built up. People will see her aura, and as Tami she can't walk that far!"

Mac laughed. "Marie, she's the strongest Synon. She'll find a way. Just relax and watch for her."

Marie sighed. "Okay." She sat in thought waiting for Tami. It must be irritating for Synons to go through the process of speaking language out loud. Their telepathy must be at the speed of light, she mused. I need to ask Jeff about that. But he's human. He probably has to telepath at the pace of verbal thought. Weird.

She wasn't thrilled about having to drive back alone in the car with Tami. Marie wasn't sure she'd ever be able to warm to her, even though she was certain that Tami regretted the way she had used Jeff when they first met and was sincere in her assertion that Marie and Jeff belonged together.

It didn't seem like much time had elapsed before Tami Graves appeared at her car window, wearing a big smile. "Hi Marie. It's good to see you. Can I put my bag in the back?"

A bit startled, it took Marie a moment to respond. Tami had even remembered to manufacture a bag. "Sure. I'll open the hatch." In the rearview mirror, she watched the tall, willowy figure glide toward the trunk, long auburn hair blowing in the breeze, displaying bright red shafts as the sun reflected off it. Marie felt a pang of jealousy. Tami wore the appearance of Jeff's adolescent dream woman, which she had plucked from his sleeping mind. Marie looked very different—petite, with hair she described as dirty blond, cut in a short bob. She knew Jeff loved her; they were best friends and what Tami called soulmates. It was silly to feel resentment at Tami's choice of persona. After all, it had brought the Synons into Jeff's life and led to what appeared to be his destiny.

Tami climbed into the passenger seat. "If I were human, I'd be exhausted," she exclaimed. "Arduous is a mild word to describe my trip from the river. I'm just glad for clumps of greenspace here, along with animals connected to The Living World, to provide help to Synons traveling incognito."

Marie grinned. "Maybe Mac should have asked me to drive to the river instead of having you hop your way here by whatever Passageways you could scrounge up."

"So right. Synon intelligence isn't always as practical as that of humans. "Well, I can't wait to get into the mountains and see this new camp."

Marie had backed out as they chatted and was waiting at the light to enter a main road. She was surprised at the ease in which they had launched into a conversation. She realized that she actually liked Tami Graves a little bit.

■　　■　　■

As Marie and Tami drove to the Tech Center and chatted, another part of Tami's mind was chewing on the Bandela mystery. The assault on the Realm had come from Earth. Its purpose was obviously to provide a distraction to enable Bandela's escape; that meant a Passageway. He had help from renegades on Earth. Find his renegade helpers and she'd find Bandela.

She thought back to the night they had subdued Bandela. While he confronted the Synons, his renegade supporters had hung back in the shadows. Once he was in custody, most of them were remorseful, begging for amnesty. They had been sent back to the Realm to be observed as efforts were made to rehabilitate them. Some had obviously slipped away in the darkness and chaos. Her thoughts went to Bret and his group. They hadn't been with Bandela then, but she and MacIntyre had caught them trying to close a Passageway. Even though their objectives were different, they might align with Bandela to take advantage of his strength, knowledge, and abilities. They were strong and advanced and had probably regained power to transform from the rabbit personas she had imposed on them. By now, they would have escaped the animal refuge where she had left them. They were a good place to start. If she could find them.

■　　■　　■

"Tami!" Emma ran toward the beautiful woman walking towards them with Marie. "You came to visit!" Emma wrapped her arms around Tami. A strong bond had been forged between them after Emma's rescue.

Tami embraced the girl, kissing the top of her head and murmuring, "Emma! I'm so proud of you!"

When they finally disengaged, Emma exclaimed, "I went through Passageways!" She sobered. "Well, actually, Judilay and Annilu took me through them. I couldn't have done it on my own."

"I knew you were capable of doing it, just like Jeff. And, yes, we're fortunate to have Annilu and Judilay. They have worked hard to refine their processes." Tami turned to the larger group that had been sitting around a fire pit as the setting sun painted the western sky pink and blue. She found the two Synons who were being discussed and offered them her dazzling smile. Both looked a little abashed.

Rick and Tina hung back. Although they had heard some of the stories about Emma's adventure, they were shy in the presence of this figure they knew was the human persona of TuMa'Aye Gra'Vay.

Jeff spoke up. "Uniques, I'd like to formally introduce Tami Graves. Rick, Tina." Tami nodded and smiled at each. She sank into a chair. "I'll repeat to you what I told Marie: If I were human, I'd be wiped out."

Laughter erupted, breaking the ice. A comfortable conversation got underway until Lew's voice boomed. "The cook just poked her head out the door to summon us in for dinner. Let's enjoy it."

■　　■　　■

Dinner was lively. Judilay was the only quiet one. Lana watched him, wondering what was going through his mind. She knew what was in hers. Strong mixed emotions. A warm friendship had blossomed between them. She was already missing him, even though she was happy he was getting what he wanted so badly. Lana wished he'd take this chance to announce where he was going and why. She gave him a nudging look. He nodded and looked at Mac for a moment.

Mac's loud voice cut through the clamor. "Folks, I think Judilay might want to tell you something." He looked at the young dark-skinned persona wearing dreadlocks and a colorful dashiki.

Judilay nodded. "Yes. I've been trying to find a way to make this announcement." The room quieted, as concerned expressions broke out. "It's good news, but a bit sad for me as well. Those who have known me since I arrived are aware that I am eager to travel, to meet and learn from diverse people. Mac has graciously arranged for that to begin. I'm leaving in a few days for the Bahamas."

A shock went through the Tech Team who had become fond of Judilay and accustomed to his presence. Annilu sat expressionless. After only a moment of silence, congratulations and good wishes surrounded Judilay. He continued. "I'll be an intern with a conservation organization. It's a perfect opportunity to travel throughout the Caribbean. I can learn about the cultures and environments while educating people on effective ways to protect their environments and improve their standard of living. But I'll sure miss all of you. I'm so thankful for the time I had with you here and for all the help you've given me."

Jeff stood, holding his glass of iced tea. "A toast to our good friend and colleague."

All lifted their glasses, some clinking them together. "On a personal note," Jeff's voice softened. "I'm a better person for the time I've spent with Judilay. I'll miss you, my friend."

Mannie Patel lifted the mood by interjecting his trademark wry humor. "Jeff, you're lucky. For you, he's an instant away by telepathy. The rest of us mere humans will have to rely on electronics." An eyebrow rose. "Just you keep that mobile charged down there."

Lana struggled to hold back tears.

■   ■   ■

Judilay reclined, feet up, arms behind his head, soaking up the warm sun and cooling Bahamian breeze. A broad, unbidden smile erupted across his face. Convinced that he felt emotional responses, he thought that he was possibly unique among Synons. While other Synons were adept at simulating emotion in their interactions with people, it was not one of their attributes. They were imbued with universal ethics that allowed them to make decisions and take actions for the greater good, and when appropriate, for the benefit of individuals. They were innately empathetic, but unlike people, they weren't driven by emotions and impulses that could affect consequences. Even though Judilay continued to function within these parameters, he had experienced reactions to events and circumstances that he could only call emotional responses.

When researching potential persona attributes, he had been especially attracted to the Caribbean cultures, the history of its people, and environments. It had prompted the look in which he felt so comfortable. Judilay had only been to Earth a few times previously for short durations. He had urged the Realm to give him a chance to prove his worth through the assignment with MacIntyre that originally had focused on communicating with Earth to find ways to help her.

Judilay's ambitions had convinced them to send him along with the equally strong and inexperienced Annilu. The persona choices and behaviors of the two proved to be very different. As the leader of the mission, and longtime observer of human behavior and interaction, MacIntyre recognized Judilay's value and approved the transfer to the Caribbean. His only restriction was that Judilay's first assignment be to an English-speaking location. Synons could rapidly learn new languages, but Mac didn't want that extra factor to inhibit Judilay's ability to immediately begin interacting with people through his capacity to build trust and friendship.

Now Judilay was settling into his new location and job. It had been a shock to experience a wistful pang when saying good-bye to his human friend Lana Adams at the Tech Center. All the tech team had hugged him, but when Lana embraced and released him, his head seemed to swim as feelings washed over him; he felt the same emotions in her that he was experiencing. He recalled the dinner at which he announced his impending departure. A look from Lana seemed to plant the notion in his mind that prompted him to telepath Mac for permission to speak to the group. She had displayed no telepathic abilities. Judilay thought they might be experiencing the kind of bond that grew between people.

Judilay knew a little of the relationship that had developed between Tami Graves and Jeff Hawke. However, it had been deliberately instigated as part of TuMa'Aye Gra'Vay's plan and the Tami persona designed to unconsciously appeal to Jeff. The friendship that sprang up between Judilay and Lana had been spontaneous. He now admitted to himself that he had immediately felt drawn to her, which at the time he simply attributed to her being similar in appearance and cultural background to his chosen persona. As exciting as the new experiences here were, he kept wishing she were there to share them. He had already sent her a flurry of texts and photos to which she enthusiastically responded. Was there some undisclosed plan for the two of them? Or was he evolving?

CHAPTER SEVEN

Bandela-Jackson didn't believe the planetary scientist's spiel. Maybe humans, and their equipment, couldn't accurately measure it, but to him, Earth's rotation was constantly erratic. After he joined up with his main contingent of supporters, he would find solitude and investigate. His strength and perception were stronger than most other Synons, nevertheless, he would consult with this group that had been on Earth for many years, especially their leader, Bret.

Bandela-Jackson was irritated that the humans were so stupid. If they allowed the planet to become uninhabitable in the near future, as seemed their path, it could literally destroy the Synons whose existence depended on the link of Earth's inhabitants to Nature and on to the Realm.

An alternate option to ruling over humans from the internet was to live within a robotic body. That would require minions to maintain the body and its power sources. He needed to ascertain how damaged Earth was. He was even prepared to help, if possible, to enable his future plans, possibly even his survival.

His renegades had resided close to where Bandela as Dr. Jackson had worked in North Carolina's Research Triangle and led his own gang to invade a local municipality's computer network, providing him with a vast store of knowledge. His followers had stayed in the shadows during the nocturnal confrontation in which Bandela was subdued by the Synons, slipping away to avoid capture. Fortunately, he had discovered Bret and his group who led his rescue from his prison in the Realm. They had moved to the coastal region, which although developed, offered more hidden wilderness spots. Bret invited Bandela-Jackson to join them there.

Bret had bought an expanse of undeveloped land at auction. Even though a large popular lake wasn't far away, their land was heavily overgrown and only accessible by a couple of unpaved roads. The renegades could nestle in without ever being noticed.

It was an adjustment for Bandela-Jackson to live in such a remote area. However, it kept him hidden and offered secluded places to sound out what was happening with Earth. As soon as he was settled in the small house Bret had built for him, he told them he needed time to contemplate and went into the woods.

Jackson, as Bandela was growing more comfortable inhabiting again, could move much faster than his persona should be able to if he were human. He jogged through stands of pine trees and thick underbrush until he found a small clearing that sloped down to a swamp. He transformed and burrowed into the soft ground. Insects and small creatures invaded his mind; he mentally swatted them away. Focusing narrowly, his mind bore downward. He had already become acclimated to the lurching rotation and now concentrated on reaching for the planet's core. His mind was assailed with a jumble of negative images and feelings. Earth was, indeed, under strain. In eons past, he had learned how to link with Earth. The experience had always been one of awe at the humming efficiency that touched every particle of the planet and orchestrated interdependent systems, engendering flourishing ecosystems supporting myriad lifeforms. Now, there was no rhythmic hum, only what his mind perceived as chaos, swirling within a weakened state.

Bandela sent a mental message, not in words, but of concepts, inquiring what he could do to be of assistance. Feeble impressions reached him that seemed to carry the words "they must help." Then the link with Earth was severed.

Bandela swirled into the swamp, floating above the water lapping around cypress trees. Did he really perceive those words? Who were "they?" He could only conclude Earth referred to Synons. Who else could it possibly be?

One afternoon, Jackson, Bret and several others were outside attempting to use devices they had rigged up to measure Earth's rotational rhythm. A Passageway abruptly opened in the nearby woods from which Akari emerged, instantly transforming to her persona. The group greeted her and invited her to join them.

Jackson intervened. "She's been on a mission for me. I need to debrief her privately. You keep working on this while Akari and I take a walk in the forest."

They moved silently until they were away from the group. Jackson telepathed to Akari, "Close your mind to all but me. They can easily eavesdrop on us." She nodded. He went on speaking mentally to her. "Have you made a report to Singleton yet?"

"No. I thought I should check in with you first. I had little result. Kurosawa had no contact data for Jeff McCarthy or any of his associates. After initial friendliness, she became suspicious of me and moved to another location. I tried visiting her there, but she brushed me off."

Jackson displayed a very human scowl. "Perhaps you need more training."

Her countenance hardened. "I have more training and experience than you in covert operations. I think this woman was tipped off somehow."

Jackson's eyebrows rose. "Quite interesting. That indicates that she is in communication with someone who identified you, possibly through the televised images I observed in which you carelessly allowed yourself to appear."

Akari was clearly insulted. "Her crew roamed around constantly shooting footage. Who would recognize me from imagery? I haven't had an operation in a long time using this persona."

Jackson pondered for long moments. "That can be our answer. You must retrace your activities and account for people and Synons who might have encountered you, or that you investigated. That can tell us who Kurosawa works with."

Akari was loathe to agree with him but recognized his point. "I'll retreat and reconstruct my missions. But before doing so, shouldn't I report to Singleton?"

"Unfortunately, yes. First, let's review how you came in contact with him. There might be leads there."

Akari nodded and began speaking, "Singleton has a network of contacts and operatives he can call on for information and to conduct assignments. Although relatively large and spread out, it is tight knit, held together not by camaraderie but by intimidation. They all carry considerable guilt and wield it over each other. It took me some time to penetrate, utilizing my own associations, until I found a common link.

"I spied on Singleton." She stopped and spat in human fashion. "His mind is dark, although brilliant. I learned of his obsession with Kurosawa, Jeff McCarthy, and the supposed aliens." She barked a laugh. So I then moved my spy operation to her. I did find experiences in her mind with Jeff McCarthy and the kidnapped girl, but not with aliens or Synons. I discovered that she was going to Japan so immediately spread the word that I was available for work there. It didn't take long for Singleton to contact me. Of course, he has no notion that I am anything other than a human operative for hire."

Jackson smiled. His mind whirled. "I need to string him along. Telephone him. Here's what to say."

* * *

While Tami enjoyed meeting the Uniques and seeing the progress made at the Camp, she was eager to get on with her search for Bandela. She conferred with the other Synons there. It seemed unlikely that Bandela would try to revert to his Dr. Gabe Jackson life, since that would enable them to easily locate him. Seeking out Bret and the former "biker-bunnies" seemed the most effective path. As they had been in the same Research Triangle area as Bandela-Jackson, it was likely that they had at least crossed paths with him. They were extremely strong and advanced so would be useful contacts for Bandela now. They were adept at blocking their signatures from detection by other Synons and would be difficult to locate. Tami decided to talk to other Triangle Earth-Synons. Lew wanted to visit the Native American Cultural Center he had left in the hands of a Synon known as Aden, a Cherokee woman, who had been his assistant.

When Marie offered to drive them so that she could also visit friends, Tami immediately suggested, "Let's stay at the bed and breakfast Jeff's cousin Sarah owns. I'd love to see her again. And the Dream Catcher is so lovely."

Marie brightened. "Great idea! I really like her, and you're right, it's the perfect place for us. I'll call and arrange it."

Lew looked wistful. "As fond as I am of Sarah, I'd prefer to stay at the center. I need to find out what assistance Aden might need, and a circle of Earth-Synons hang around there that will be helpful for our mission."

CHAPTER EIGHT

Returning to the Dream Catcher dredged up memories for Tami. She once again experienced tumult indicating that her persona had developed something akin to emotions. She was glad to have Marie's company.

It was wonderful to see Sarah Hawke again. Although it had barely been a little over a year since Tami had left here, she noticed strands of silver in Sarah's thick brown hair that formed a wide halo around her face. The broad smile was the same, as was the affectionate embrace into which Sarah drew both Tami and Marie.

"How did you two link up?" Sarah asked.

Tami quickly answered, aware that Sarah had no knowledge of Synons or of her cousin Jeff's abilities. "Through Jeff initially. Then just recently Marie and I happened to run into each other in Asheville. I met up with Lew and the team at the Tech Center and the three of us decided to make this trip."

Marie grinned brightly, remaining silent.

"Fantastic! Come on in. I know you're tired. I'll take you to your rooms." Her long colorful skirt swished as she turned and led them down the hall.

Memories of her first visit here floated around Tami. That trip had set in motion everything that had happened the past two years. A shudder wracked her as she recalled her battle with Bandela and his Synon renegades by the backyard pond. She wondered if those same companions were with him now.

■　■　■

Nostalgia gripped Lewis Henderson as he was warmly welcomed back to the Native American Cultural Center he had founded and expanded to serve as a shelter for the unhoused when they were threatened by bad weather. The center was an activity center for the transitional community in which it nestled, as well as a museum and resource center for at least eight North Carolina Indian tribes.

Aden had done a phenomenal job of maintaining and enhancing the center. Lew quickly summoned the Earth-Synons who also served as center volunteers. They met late in the evening after closing. All retained the personas which had become natural to them as they sat in comfortable old chairs in the library. These had formed the backbone of the Synon contingent that Tami had led into a computer network in their energy forms to battle Bandela and his renegades.

Lew basked in the contented glow for a while, then soberly spoke. "Bandela has escaped from the Realm—" He was interrupted by gasps and exclamations. "He had help from his followers here. We need to find out where he is and what he's up to."

Aden nodded. "We tried to keep tabs on the old renegade bunch. They seemed to go into hiding after he was taken away. Vanished."

"What about the biker gang led by an Earth-Synon called Bret?"

An older woman, spoke up. "I heard tales." She chuckled. "I think you know what happened to them." She glared at Lew then smiled slyly. "Bunnies?"

Lew laughed out loud. "Okay. We need to know where they went."

She nodded. "They never returned to their old warehouse home. Without their concentrated power, the furnishings they'd maintained reverted to their original forms that filled it with detritus. We weren't able to get any residual signatures from it before the owners cleaned it out and rented it again."

One of the men interjected. "We can casually ask around. Put out the word that someone has a job for them."

"Good plan. Let's get it into action right away." Lew was pleased. He knew this group would come through. They had established a widespread network of operatives and spies. He got up slowly in the manner of the old man he impersonated. "Now I've got to pretend to be a human and have dinner at the Dream Catcher with Sarah and Marie, and, of course, Tami."

■　　■　　■

It took little time for the Earth-Synons to learn where Bret had gone. Word was that the group had moved somewhere on the coast around Wilmington. That entailed a wide area, but was a good starting point. A few of the closer ones would try to find their exact location.

Mac had told Marie to take a little vacation while the Tech Center could spare her. Marie had mixed feelings about it. More and more, she felt like a bystander instead of being involved in the vital work that was being done, nevertheless, she was tired and relished the thought of free time away from the tension.

Relaxing at the Dream Catcher was inviting. After arriving and settling in, Marie had thought about catching up with friends but realized there could be too many questions she was unable to answer about why they had moved away and what they were doing. It would be difficult enough to meet Sarah's curiosity.

When the three of them discussed what to tell Sarah, Tami told Marie, "If you need to go back, go ahead. I'm prone to flitting around where I'm needed. Lew is staying a while longer to help out at the center. I'll tell Sarah I just got an assignment that will take me away. Remember, she thinks I'm a magazine writer."

The next day the three women had one last dinner together. Sarah insisted on preparing a sumptuous picnic to enjoy on her deck. It was relaxing looking over her garden with the pond glistening beyond. It was a secluded refuge within a busy city.

Marie noticed that Tami kept glancing toward the pond. "Is this a natural pond?" Marie asked Sarah.

"Yes. It's the main reason the inn was originally built here." She gazed toward the bucolic view of trees and flowers thriving right up to the water's edge. "It's what drew my uncle to buy it." She paused a moment in thought. "There are ancient legends about that pond. One in particular recounts a fierce battle between the forces of good and evil. I don't recall the details. I think a shaman was attacked by a demon, or something similar. I don't know if the legends have Native American roots or not."

Tami was peering intently at Sarah. "You can't recall anything more?" There was an urgent edge to her voice.

"No. I'm sorry. There might be some information at the center."

"Thanks. I'll ask Lew to check on it. It intrigues me." Tami's gaze was intent as it again settled on the pond.

Then it hit Marie. Tami had told them Bandela had attacked her behind the Dream Catcher. Marie locked eyes with Tami, but the Synon quickly looked away, eyes glazing over.

■　■　■

Tami's focus wavered. She was having trouble maintaining her persona. The vision of her two companions fluctuated; they were fading away. Her perspective flowed in slow motion; she felt like she was traversing a Passageway. Abruptly, the world became clear again; she was moving. Tami looked back and saw no lawn, no building, no people, no sights, sounds or smells of the urban setting where she had been. As far as her Synon sight extended there was only arid, cracked land bereft of vegetation. No animal minds touched hers. No buzz of insects. The pond, if that was what it was, had shrunk to a mere puddle, covered in pungent slime. A cloudless sky bore a grayish tint, despite the glaring hot sun.

Tami realized that she was no longer Tami. She was her true self, TuMa'Aye Gra'Vay, with no material aspect. Her aura glowed and pulsated. Was she still on Earth? And if so, where and when?

Abruptly her surroundings darkened. A vast shadow blocked the light. In the distance could be heard the scraping howls of tectonic plates shifting. She felt the Earth teeter on the brink of halting her rotation. Her mind summoned fellow Synons. No response. No enveloping Realm! Emptiness! Total void! She was alone! Her energy was diminishing and with it her mind and spirit, her conscious link to The Living World. TuMa'Aye Gra'Vay, strongest of her kind, focused her waning consciousness into the dry, hard dirt that clothed what remained of the living Earth. Down she bore, through what had been complex layers of rock, mineral, water, touching the faintest warmth of magma where there should be a roaring furnace. Memories sprang up of the desperate attempts by Synon and Unique humans to reach Earth, and the faint responses that filled their minds with pleas for help.

The effort was dissipating what power she had left. She persisted. If she were the last of her kind she would give what was left of herself to become one with the dying planet that had been the very purpose for her existence.

◼ ◼ ◼

"Tami! Tami! She vanished!" Sarah ran to the chair where Tami Graves had sat a moment before. She dove into the chair, kneeling in it, pounded its back, sinking her face into the cushion. Marie grappled with her own shock, her first responder training kicking in to push emotions aside, grasping for reason. She fought not to think of the implications of what had just happened. Sarah was the priority. The trauma she experienced would rapidly cause her to question her own sanity.

Marie grabbed the phone from her pocket and called Lewis Henderson.

"Marie! What happened?" His usually languid voice carried an urgent, demanding tone, his keen abilities warning that Marie was in distress.

"Tami vanished!" She rushed to quell his response. "Sarah saw it! She's in shock. I don't want to call an ambulance. How could I explain what happened?" She absently noticed that tears were streaming down her face.

"No people!" It was a command. "Try to calm her and tell her Tami probably just took a walk and you two didn't notice. I'll send over someone with medical training. I must go. All Synons are linking to search for TuMa'Aye."

◼ ◼ ◼

After comprehensive plans were discussed and analyzed, groups of Synons were assigned to search the Realm and Earth in grid patterns, focusing on various places of high probability. Several weeks passed with no results. It was like the Tami Graves persona had simply vanished, just as her human friend, Sarah Hawke, described seeing occur.

The search continued. The Earth was replete with places she could be, of course; but why couldn't they find her signature? Why wasn't she broadcasting for help if she needed it? What power was greater than TuMa'Aye Gra'Vay? The Living World. Quiet, shielded discussions were held among Tork, Mac and several other powerful Synons who tended to lead the less experienced in dealing with Earth and its multitude of issues. Why would The Living World intervene so suddenly with no warning to them? Had they failed? Were they to blame for what was happening to Earth? It was as dark a time as their long memories could recall.

CHAPTER NINE

Jeff felt like a spectator on the sidelines of extraordinary events. He had busied himself working with the children. They were frustrated by the slow pace of their training and the lack of new Uniques at the camp. The three kids were doing so well that Jeff thought they could benefit from working on their own a few days. He decided to take a solo camping trip farther into the mountain wilderness. Mac thought it was a good idea, so Jeff made his plan, gathered his provisions, and set out.

The transition from summer to autumn was beginning. In the highest elevations of deciduous forests leaves were starting to bring out their seasonal gold, red, and orange hues. Nights were cooler; the sky was clear, revealing the Earth's home galaxy, the Milky Way, in all its star-studded glory.

Jeff realized how much he had missed solitary time in Nature. He felt closer to Earth than ever; his heart tugged at the thought of her plight. On the second night, after he had eaten, Jeff climbed up to a granite outcrop above his campsite. He felt like part of the expansive sky rather than the Earth on which he sat. He slipped into a trance and found himself floating in the sky, looking down on the curve of the planetary horizon. He was just one of a multitude of twinkling stars. Jeff soared higher and higher, watching his body sitting on the rock become smaller. His soaring mind left Earth's atmosphere. It was so thin! Such a fragile protection for Earth and her life! He nearly collided with a large object—a man-made satellite! He was surrounded by them in all directions, mingled with chunks of debris. He floated above it all. He had no eyes, but was able to somehow perceive like he did in his body. Jeff had only seen Earth from this perspective in photographs. He recalled the historic ones taken from the moon by American astronauts. Jeff saw the globe of the Earth, half covered with the glow of electric lights amid darkness, the other half illuminated by the rays of the sun, filtered by that thin veil of protective atmosphere. Without conscious intent, Jeff broadcast the image he perceived, like a television signal routed across the globe.

■   ■   ■

Across Earth Synon minds were invaded with Jeff's imagery. It was so abrupt that they struggled to control their reactions. Was this somehow connected to TuMa'Aye Gra'Vay's recent disappearance? Did she send the image? Many who had been interacting with people tried to quickly cover up their reactions by mumbled things like, "I just had a sudden dizzy spell," or "Sorry, my mind wandered a moment." Those not in the company of humans turned their full attention to the sudden vision. Jeff's transmission was so strong that the Realm shuddered and crackled with power as its inhabitants shared the experience and sought to trace its origin. Was it TuMa'Aye attempting to reach them?

■   ■   ■

Mac immediately knew that the experience was emanating from Jeff, but decided not to reveal that to the other camp residents. The kids had received it, but not the other people there, so he surmised that Uniques and Synons were the only recipients. He knew his group needed some kind of explanation, so after quickly conferring with Annilu, he arranged a meeting with the people to explain what he could.

■   ■   ■

The exhausted children had just hit their pillows. Since there were only three of them, they had the luxury of private rooms meant for future instructors. Stunned, they all ran out into the hall babbling at each other.

It was Mannie Patel's turn to sleep in another of the rooms as an adult supervisor. The commotion sent him dashing to his door, grabbing a bathrobe as he opened it. The kids were gathered in the hall, all talking at the same time. It was apparent that something unusual had happened. "Kids!" He bellowed. "Quiet down and tell me what's going on!" The children abruptly shut up and gawked at him like he was a strange interloper.

Emma stepped toward him, her face pale in the dim night-lights that lined the hall. "Vision," she muttered. "Did you see it?"

"No." Mannie wished he'd remembered to grab his phone.

"Wait." Emma held up her arm. Her eyes went blank a few moments. The other children stood huddled together behind her, all assuming the same unfocused gaze.

Great, Mannie thought. They're all getting a message. He felt useless.

"Everybody just chill!" Emma shouted. The children had begun excitedly talking again. "Don't be so rude to our friend Mannie." She looked at him as he stood in his robe wearing a perplexed and irritated expression. "Sorry," she said to him. "We all had some kind of shared experience that was totally unbelievable. Mac wants us all to meet in the gathering hall. It will take a few minutes for the others to get there, so we might as well use the time to put on our regular clothes." She grinned as her eyes swept over the other two kids who stood there in pajamas.

"Am I invited?" Mannie asked.

"Of course! So, you'd better put on some clothes too."

Around the globe, there were people shocked by the sudden vivid image. Uniques unaware of their power had suspected that they were somehow different but fell back on varied rationales to dismiss random telepathic events they couldn't explain. Others who felt strongly that they had extrasensory powers had simply lacked verification. As they all abruptly found themselves sharing Jeff's experience, they reacted in a myriad ways. Those who were sleeping attributed the experience to vivid dreams. Those who were engaged in solitary activities stopped, like the Synons, trying to observe and analyze while experiencing the image. Those who were engaged with others attempted to push it aside as if it hadn't happened, hoping their strange behavior hadn't been noticed. At first, few dared mention it to anyone else. However, some saw it as such an unusual experience that they felt compelled to share it, especially for those who saw it as validation of their suspicion that they had special capabilities.

The Synons recognized that this shared experience could rapidly spread across social media, and from there to news outlets. They were forced to turn their focus from the search for TuMa'Aye to this new emergency. They conferred, constructing plans to mitigate panic, or worse, revelation of telepathy among humans, a topic that required delicate treatment. This sudden situation forced rapid action.

* * *

"How could he have done that?" Tork's voice reverberated in every Synon mind.

Mac responded. "I've known from the beginning that Jeff was extremely unique. He could have power far beyond other human telepaths."

They were stunned by Jeff's mental voice, dripping with sarcasm. "Thanks for talking about me like I couldn't hear you."

Mac retorted, "Have you always been able to listen in on private Synon conversations?"

"Don't know. The Tower of Babel just appeared in my head. I was able to filter out most of it, but you guys were so loud that I couldn't get rid of you. May I speak?"

"Please do!" Tork actually shouted.

"There's no way I can apologize for what I did. It was an uncontrollable impulse. I guess I was just so overwhelmed with the experience that I sent it out. I had no idea how far it went."

Mac boomed, "Every Unique on Earth is overwhelmed! Confused! Terrified!"

"Aw, man! I think I was so awed by how wondrous the Earth is—but also how vulnerable it looks just hanging in space. I guess my unconscious felt the urge to share it."

Mac interjected. "I'm sitting here on Earth surrounded by the only three Uniques that we know are aware of their own powers. It's ironic that we're searching so hard to ferret out others, only to have them become aware all at once. Jeff, we'll deal with you later. Right now every Synon, especially those on Earth, must send out messages asking all those people who received the images to respond." he paused. "How? Should we set up a website? Establish meeting places? Ideas?"

Jeff answered, "They'll be most comfortable with a website app. I'll get the team on that as soon as I can get to cell and internet service. I'll leave when it's light enough to find my way out. It will take a little time. I just recall how shocked I was when I first heard Emma's voice in my head, but then I was elated. Now I'm thinking Uniques will feel like they shared something extremely special and important. We just need to stop them from blabbing about it to non-Uniques. Isn't that paramount right now?"

Annilu was emboldened to speak. "Maybe another blast, perhaps from Tork?"

Tork's voice stated, "Jeff. It has to be Jeff."

Mac replied, "Absolutely."

"Should I astral travel again? Is that possibly what allowed my message to be so potent?"

Tork was astonished. "You astral traveled?"

"That's the only way I could describe it. I saw my body sitting on a rock, but my consciousness was in the sky intact with physical senses."

An unfamiliar voice interrupted. "Hello, I'm Asya, a Synon in Turkey. Could I return to the issue of the other Uniques?" Silent assent led her to continue. "We're a group working with others globally to establish databases of Earth-Synons and potential Uniques. We have an untested procedure for texting group messages. We can test it with a blast to those we are virtually certain are Uniques. We just need a message."

Mutually observed silent contemplation ensued for long moments, broken by Tork. "We have two proposals. Should we implement both?"

It was decided that the first step was to establish the website, after which both communications methods would be used.

Mac asked, "Jeff, do you think you can astral travel again closer to the Tech Center?"

"I don't know. If I can talk to you guys in the Realm and across Earth, I should be able to do it again. If I need inspiration, there are some spectacular vistas nearby. All I can do is try."

█   █   █

Bandela-Jackson had been stunned by Jeff's image and now was flabbergasted that he was a recipient of the linked Synon discussions. He was confident that his strong shielding and the sheer number of Synons on the link would prevent him from being discovered. He wanted to know more, so he remained a silent listener. Could there actually be numerous humans who could communicate telepathically with each other and Synons? If so, they could pose a threat to his long-range plans.

Then there was still the lingering absence of TuMa'Aye Gra'Vay. There had been a flurry of Synon activity when she abruptly disappeared. That was a mystery. He knew how strong and resourceful she was. One part of him was relieved that she was gone; another part was apprehensive. Any force that could remove her from the Realm and the Earth could probably accomplish anything. He smiled. The most likely answer was that she herself had taken some action that hid her, even from her own kind, and for her own purpose.

He shivered. The only power great enough to cause TuMa'Aye Gra'Vay to disappear was The Living World.

█   █   █

Leaving his campsite at first light, Jeff was uneasy. The kids would have got his image along with the Synons at the camp. Did they recognize that it was from him? The Tech Team had to be told what had happened in order to quickly set up the website. He had to assume that when he arrived everyone would know. What he really wanted to do was just hide out in the mountains. But he had to own up to what he had done and take whatever steps he could to mitigate it and salvage any benefits it might bring. He was curious to learn how many people had actually received his broadcasted image. That might be the upside to his grave error. They could now connect with the Uniques. Could they take advantage in time to help Earth?

He drove straight to the Tech Center. Shower and clean clothes had to wait. He found the team, Mac and Lew in the central work area. The people all stood around awkwardly looking at him in awe. He grinned and nodded toward them as Marie moved to gently embrace him. Lew followed with his own embrace.

Mac scowled and started a rapid discourse. "I briefed the team on what we must do. They've already begun the basic website construction and are researching the best URL name for it. We should work on the content of your next broadcast." Jeff nodded. Somehow he couldn't find his voice.

Lew suggested that they go into one of the closed offices to work on the message while the team continued with the website. Jeff was very uncomfortable knowing that Mac was furious with him. When they were settled, with Jeff at the computer to take notes and work on the message composition, Mac began dictating to him.

Settling on wording that was concise and clear took some time. Jeff directed his full attention to the work by using his practiced method of pushing away emotions. They had the message complete and ready to insert the website address before the team had finished establishing the site.

Jeff said tersely, "I need to shower and change. I can work on memorizing this at home until the web information is ready." He headed for the door.

As he passed, Lew caught his arm. "Jeff, this might prove to be exactly what we needed. Our priority now is to contact and bring in as many new Uniques as possible. They'll need help; and Earth needs them."

Jeff nodded and left the room.

When he walked into the cabin Cosmos appeared, rubbing his head against Jeff's legs as his body wound its way around them. Jeff bent to stroke the silky head. "Thanks for the welcome, friend," he murmured. A feeling of love swept through him. Just being back in his comforting home soothed him.

Jeff showered, dressed, and stretched out on the bed with the printout of his speech to learn it; Cosmos curled up next to him, purring. Jeff studied the short speech, committing it to memory before sleep overtook him.

■　　■　　■

Jeff was alone at a place he and Marie had stumbled across while exploring. A path led up from a narrow road bordering a ridgeline with a drop-off and vista on the side opposite the path that wound upward to the crest and an even more spectacular vista.

Jeff found a boulder to sit on. He hoped he could again fall into the trance that took his mind aloft. He stared at the vista that looked like a sea of mountains. Peering downward he could see a colorful patchwork of cultivated fields. The sky was what some called "Carolina blue" dotted with a few wispy white clouds. The sun was behind him, casting shafts of light along slopes on which a medley of colorful trees was illuminated. It was easy for Jeff's body to relax and his mind wander as serenity engulfed him.

Again, he marveled at how rapidly he left the Earth and its fragile atmosphere beneath him. He realized that he could direct his consciousness. He moved farther away until the entire globe was in view. Gathering his power to broadcast the message, Jeff aimed his mind at the Realm and the Earth. He wondered if the Uniques who received it would hear a voice that sounded human or experience non-lingual thoughts. Would they hear their own language? He sent his message. "You aren't crazy or being attacked. You and I are among some people with telepathic abilities. Recently, while meditating, my mind traveled far above Earth. I was so awe-stricken with what I saw that I projected the image telepathically, and you were able to receive it. Please don't share your experience publicly. It can alarm others. We have a secure website to give you information, links, and phone numbers to people who can help you." He sent the address of the website. Jeff took a last look at the Earth and willed himself back into his body.

CHAPTER TEN

While some who got Jeff's message would eagerly access the website, others would suspect that it was a scam or something more nefarious. They would speculate that it was, among other things, a terrorist or alien attack, or an attempt by their government to identify and control them.

The Synon team led by Asya in Turkey had a more difficult challenge. Their contacts would get a text message from a strange research organization. Many would assume it was spam and delete it unread. Some mobile carriers would filter it out. Not all of the recipients would actually be telepathic, so would not have seen Jeff's projected image. It was hoped that they would delete the text as spam. Some might be curious enough to read the message, and a number among them would check out the website listed or call the number provided in the text. Someone at that number could link them to the personas of Synons they knew as people. These would be the success stories. In the meantime, those same Synons would attempt to personally contact humans they strongly felt were Uniques. The texts would also ask recipients not to publicly share their experiences.

Through both means of contacting recipients, those taking charge of the operation calculated that only a small number would respond. The attempts to reach out could backfire and prompt the sharing of stories on social media about experiencing attempts at elaborate scams, identity theft, or more farfetched conspiracy theory schemes.

Across the globe, Earth-dwelling Synons began preemptively reaching out to people most likely to be Uniques.

The Synons began preparing for widespread public coverage. Bailey MacIntyre brought in a handful of trusted humans within many governments around the world, the United Nations, science, and media who could effectively deal with the knowledge of telepaths. Planning needed to be coordinated at the highest levels to counter the expected revelation of what would certainly be dubbed "mind invasion."

A media diversion was needed. Bailey steeled himself for what he knew he must do.

■   ■   ■

"Decades! We've been friends for decades!" Vera Schechner's body was racked with sobs. Bailey MacIntyre sat, head down like a shamed boy, unable to look at her on the screen. Despite his resistance, human feelings had seeped into the makeup of his persona over his long tenure of engaging with people. Guilt, sorrow, and a myriad of other emotions seized him. Vera continued railing at him. "You couldn't trust me with the truth? Were you afraid that because I'm news director at a major network I'd be unable to keep from putting out the scoop of our age, despite the ethical concerns and potential consequences?"

Bailey managed to look at the image of her tear-stained visage. "Vera. Apologies aren't sufficient. I wanted to tell you so many times. I just didn't think it would be fair to you."

"Not fair to me! Was it fair to lead me on so long, let me hope and wish for so much more from you?" Anger and hurt swept across her face.

Bailey knew Vera had formed a strong attachment to him, which he had sought to weaken by projecting gruffness and an emphasis on the professional in their interactions. He had insisted on establishing secure communication links between them. Yet, he was aware of how much she had come to mean to him as well. It was a tragic conundrum. "I wish it could have been different, Vera. I value your friendship more than you could ever know. You've been a source of strength I relied on. I'm so sorry I took advantage of you." He straightened. "This sounds even more callous, but I've contacted you tonight because the world needs you. I can't stress the importance and urgency of this moment." Vera's eyes flickered, but her expression didn't change. He rushed ahead. "I just now gave you an abbreviated version of the story of Synon presence among people to provide you a foundation on which to formulate an immediate action plan."

Hurt filled her eyes. "Would you have ever told me about yourself if this situation hadn't forced you?"

"I don't know. I just know that this dire emergency needs your expertise, character, intellect, creativity, ability to focus and—"

"Okay." She held up her hands. "You've perked my curiosity. What the hell is happening?"

Bailey explained that it was their Synon abilities that had enabled him and his companions to discover Jeff Hawke, a very unusual person who was at the crux of the issue he had to discuss. He found it hard to tell Vera about Uniques; in their long acquaintance she had never displayed the slightest sign of being one.

He knew it would increase her distress to learn there were other people who could have relationships with him on a deeper psychic level than she ever would. He put on his sternest demeanor and rushed through the information, watching its effect play out on her countenance as she struggled to maintain composure. He then explained the accidental telepathy Jeff had sent out and its potential cascading consequences. They had to get in front of whatever media explosion ensued.

Vera sat in silence for long moments. Bailey didn't push her; he knew her mind was hard at work. When she finally spoke her tone was grave. "A couple of things. One step would be to go ahead and issue a fake story about it. I loathe the idea of being any part of that, and it could raise more questions. Reporters will try everything to dig into it. And what kind of story could you concoct, anyway? Questions about what could cause that can run to all extremes and cause panic and distrust."

Bailey nodded. "We've considered that, but we have no choice. We must come up with some proposed explanation. Believe me, the best minds are working on this, now including yours."

"Thanks. The other thing is that the first explosion will be on social media. I have little influence there. I do have one idea. A hoax. There was no image. One person or small group cooked up a hoax and posted it. Others decided to pretend they had seen it too. It spread."

"We thought of that. It could be a way to tamp down the hysteria. The bad side is that it denies the real experiences of the Uniques who received the messages. They're the people we urgently need to connect with."

"Can you explain that on the website you're setting up? Tell them we need to keep their abilities confidential for now so that they can help with the larger problems."

"Some just won't reach out. We've been concerned that Uniques who fall through the cracks will develop mental health issues. Others might lash out in various damaging ways." Now it was his turn to sit in silent contemplation. "I think we should dig into the potential threads of this scheme. I'll reach out to the others. From now on I'll include you when possible. Only a few people know our connection to this situation. Many of our Synon conclaves are mental."

"How do you keep them limited? Can you focus and direct your thoughts to specific others?"

Bailey laughed. "It's not like science fiction where telepaths constantly hear each other's thoughts. Synons automatically use certain—call them wavelengths. We can develop mental groups, like an email that includes only specific addresses. We don't even think about it; we just do it unconsciously. Human Uniques have varied levels of telepathic power. Some can't broadcast or receive very far. They all need intensive training. That's why it's so vital that we use this incident to contact them. They need help. Especially after this. Vera, I can sense fear, excitement, and mental chaos across the globe. If I let down my barriers I'd be deluged."

"Bailey, is this something that might be innate in all humans, but just not accessed by most of our brains?" Vera looked hopeful.

"We don't know. If it were possible that would totally change our action plan."

■　■　■

"No! No! No!" Emma Goodsen's eyes blazed as she stalked around the Tech Center conference room.

Mac's eyebrows knit. "It's the only viable option."

Emma glared at him. "So we abandon the Uniques that we need to save Earth!"

Lew tried to mediate. "No. No. A large global effort will reach out to them. We'll ask our people to explain to them why it's necessary to keep their abilities secret for the time being."

"By labeling them a hoax!" Jeff had never seen the girl so angry.

Rick Gomez spoke up. "I have to agree with Emma. Real Uniques will know it's a fake explanation and it'll make them paranoid. They know what they saw, but they won't trust the helpline messages. They won't respond and will just be more isolated than ever."

Slouched at the head of the table, MacIntyre's tone softened. "Thanks, kids, for being honest. My instinct to run it by you was right. Any other comments?"

The kids glanced at each other and then at Jeff. He nodded at them.

Tina was usually the quietest. Now her soft voice with its deep South accent seemed to surprise the group. "It was an amazing vision! They need to know it was real and shows that they're special. I don't think it should be called a hoax."

Jeff was coming to terms with the reality of his action and finding it easier to move forward on dealing with it. Now he beamed with pride at his charges. "So do you have any ideas of how we can head off what will happen when it gets out to the general public everywhere?"

"Wait a minute." Rick interjected. "How did we get here? We all had some kind of weird experiences."

Emma replied. "We're kids, but we shared them with someone else that we trusted. Not always our parents either."

"I thought fairies were talking to me," Emma stated.

Jeff smiled, recalling his first encounter with the girl. "All kinds of people might be Uniques. All ages. Mac, was this vision so strong that it might have touched people who just had latent telepathic abilities? Would it have been a total shock to them?"

Mac looked grave. "I'm afraid so. We don't know if our second message will reach them or not. Or if it does, if they will reach out. Some of them are the ones who will broadcast it on social media."

"They're the ones who will be most damaged by a hoax coverup," Jeff said grimly. He looked at Mac. "Do we just have to accept that we'll lose some and go ahead with the hoax plan in order to not panic everybody else?"

"We have no idea what percentage of your species is telepathic," Mac admitted. "When I brought Vera Schechner into the loop she asked if it could be latent in all humans? And in that case, might it have been triggered by this event?"

Jeff shook his head. "I think if a large percentage of people had this experience it would already be out in the open." He looked pained. "Part of me wishes everyone had it. I hate being able to have mental conversations with my cat but not my life partner."

Even though Emma and Tina were considered too young for social media, it was now included in their Unique training as part of technology training. They now took out their phones and began scrolling. "See anything yet?" Emma asked.

She was met with a negative response.

Mac grinned. "Good idea, kids. We have global teams monitoring every platform and media outlet. When something pops, we'll know it." He turned to Jeff. "So what's your opinion on a cover story?"

Jeff showed his frustration in his customary manner; he raked a hand through his hair, loudly exhaling. "I don't know. I've been thinking about what my reaction would have been if this had happened to me before I knew I was a Unique. But, you know, when the vision overtook me, I didn't immediately connect it with telepathy. It was more like I'd had an abrupt out-of-body experience. One instant I was on a rock and the next I was floating above Earth. It was only when Mac's mind interrupted that I realized it was a shared experience. So, that might be how those who received it regard it. They had a sudden—" An extraordinary thought seized his mind. His eyes widened. "Maybe I didn't do it. Maybe it was Earth." As soon as the words spilled out Jeff wished he hadn't said them. It seemed like a feeble effort to relieve him of responsibility. How could he think to blame Earth? Then a new thought took hold. Maybe it's not blaming Earth; maybe it's just accepting having been her voice.

CHAPTER ELEVEN

Suki Kurosawa had stayed in Japan as long as YCN would allow. Leaving was bittersweet. Although none of her relatives remained there, she felt like she was abandoning an ancestral home. Her crew was taking a later flight, so she embarked alone on the long trip home. Unable to focus on reading or media, she found the long, multi-leg flight back to New York provided too much time for ruminating.

It was Jack Harvey who got her the Japanese assignment for his human-interest segments. Vera Schechner had made it clear that permanent employment at YCN was no longer an option for Suki. Should she give up on national media and seek employment elsewhere? Could she adjust to reporting at a regional level, covering local stories? Would her termination from YCN impede a change?

Bitterness welled up. A few minutes of broadcasting live a five-year-old babbling about being visited by a fairy had turned out not to be fluff but had cost Suki her job. Worse, it likely put the girl on the radar of a kidnapper. Despite having worked with another reporter to locate the girl, Suki had been shut off from all information about the resolution. It was kept out of the press; as far as she could ascertain no one was ever indicted for the crime. YCN's Vera Schechner had tersely informed her that the case touched on an ongoing investigation involving multiple law enforcement agencies, and all data was classified. Suki's musing was interrupted by the announcement that they were about to land in Denver, where she had a layover.

■   ■   ■

After deplaning, Suki searched for a restaurant where she could sit comfortably while waiting for the next leg of her flight to board.

Busy perusing the businesses she passed, Suki paid little attention to the clumps of people grouped around large television screens until she found a promising restaurant and entered. Once inside, it was apparent that something was happening. Everyone stood under the wall screens from which blared a reporter's anxious voice. She joined a group to listen, but was confused by what she heard.

"What's happening?" she asked a man next to her.

"Shhh!" He admonished her.

"Okay," Suki mumbled, wandering over to another group where she found an older woman with tears running down her face. Had someone important died? She touched the woman's arm. "Excuse me. I just got off a plane. Can you tell me what's happening?"

The woman turned to her, wide-eyed. "Aliens! They've contacted us!"

"What!" Suki stared at the woman.

"Look! They're showing it!" The woman pointed to the screen.

Suki saw an image showing the Earth from space; it clearly bore a NASA logo. The reporter was narrating. "The image was similar to this one. It's unclear exactly how many people might have received it, but we know it was seen across the world. Social media is exploding with personal accounts of the image suddenly taking over people's minds, blocking out the world around them, as if they were actually floating above the Earth."

Suki moved away from the crowd, taking a seat at a table. She knew that reaching out to YCN at a time like this was useless. Scrolling through her contacts she found the number for Jeff McCarthy, the reporter she had worked with on the kidnapping. He should know something. When she called the number an automated voice directed her to leave a message. She made it as short and concise as possible.

A server had appeared with a menu that grabbed Suki's attention. She was starved for a real meal. She quickly made a choice and gave the server her order. Then she began scrolling through her social media accounts on which she followed numerous news sources. Almost all posts were about the "vision." She clicked to read the story from a reliable magazine and was surprised to learn that the initial spectacular image was followed by a message to many of the recipients providing contact information for an organization that could offer assistance. That was puzzling. She searched other posts, unsuccessfully looking for the cited contact information until her food arrived. As she ate, her analytical mind ticked away. This whole thing smelled of hoax. Every reporter and news organization in the world would be digging for answers. Whoever was able to contact the mysterious organization would have a scoop.

Suki had just ordered dessert and coffee when her phone rang. She was surprised to hear Jeff McCarthy's voice. "Hi Suki. This is Jeff. How're you doing?"

"Okay," she replied absently, eager to move on. "I've been in Japan and just now arrived at the Denver airport to see this crazy story about some alien vision. What do you know?"

His reply was firm. "Nothing. It looks like a prank, maybe a publicity stunt for a movie or something."

"From what I've seen, thousands of people saw it. How could that be done?"

He chuckled. "Way outta my league. My sources are still digging into it. It'll all come out in time. Were you in Japan on a story?"

She was irritated at his change of topic, but didn't want to be rude. He was a nice guy and a good contact. "I was. What was planned as a human-interest story at my ancestral home turned into disaster coverage when a rogue tsunami hit."

"Wow! I saw something on that. Were you there for YCN?"

"Well, my original story was slated as an online piece, but since we were on scene we were able to cover it for the network."

"Terrible for the inhabitants but a stroke of luck for you. Oh. I'm expecting a call about a job and one's coming in. Good to catch up." He disconnected.

Suki wondered if he knew more than he let on, perhaps not wanting to share anything that could be a boon for him. She lingered over coffee, then ordered an amaretto to sip while continuing to check media outlets. Finally she found one publishing the address for a website purported to be the one sent to the image recipients. She clicked on it. A message in large type appealed to anyone who had not received the image to please get off the site, as heavy traffic was slowing down aid to those who had actually seen it. At the bottom was a small arrow which she clicked. The new page contained a box directing her to answer questions in a series of fields. She sat a moment, sipping her amaretto. What she contemplated bordered on unethical. She wondered what kind of aid was being offered to those who saw the image. More importantly, who was offering it? How many other reporters were doing the same thing she was? Did they consider the ethics of their actions?

Suki bookmarked the site address and opened another browser in incognito mode. When she returned to the question box, she input information for an alias identity she sometimes used in her assignments. When she reached the question asking for her to describe exactly where she was, with whom, and what she was doing when the image appeared, she again paused. This was where she could likely be weeded out. She made it simple. She was alone, in bed, trying to fall asleep. She thought she had dozed off and had a vivid dream until the second message arrived. More questions followed, asking about details of the experience. She tried to imagine what it might have been like and concocted a story. She completed the form, giving them the address for her alias and sent it.

■　　■　　■

Suki's call aroused Jeff's suspicious nature. Should he take the time to run it by Mac? Unfortunately, someone had shared their website link for new Uniques on social media; consequently, in addition to the authentic responses, precious time was being wasted ferreting out the fakes. The authentic database was sending respondents to Earth-Synons who either knew them personally or were located close enough to meet them in person to test their telepathic abilities. Mac was overseeing the entire operation. Even with his considerable Synon abilities, his attention was stretched thin.

Deciding not to bother Mac, Jeff turned his focus back to work, but the call continued to nag at him until his intuition told him he had to tell MacIntyre.

"I was aware of it," his friend's voice was calm in his mind.

"What? With everything going on?"

"You have a special spot in my awareness." With a smile, Jeff pictured Mac's droll visage. "A good percentage of our fakes are reporters trying to find out who's on the other end. We're rewording the contact forms." In his customary style, Mac abruptly cut the link.

■   ■   ■

Suki was uncharacteristically nervous sitting across from the older woman who had yet to introduce herself. Her eyes seemed to penetrate to Suki's soul. Nevertheless, the woman projected warmth as she idly fingered her long necklace of varied semi-precious stones. Suki pegged her as perhaps well-positioned in a corporate setting—not what Suki had expected. The meeting place was odd as well—a cramped space within a "rent-an-office" site. The woman spoke. "Why are you wasting our valuable time?"

Suki was shocked by the woman's directness. She hesitated, gathering her thoughts. How had they tracked her? Had her alias been compromised? It had to be her laptop. She had neglected to activate her VPN and used the restaurant Wi-Fi, which led them to her. She was angry at herself for the lapse. Was she in danger now? Was the website a police dragnet to draw in criminals? There was no use in denial. She met the woman's gaze. "I apologize. I'm a reporter. You probably know that. I was just hoping to find information on a baffling situation."

"If we were ready to speak to the press, we would have taken the initiative. Our instructions were to not share information."

"It's all over social media. You know, I've had some dealings with local and federal law enforcement. Did you find me through my laptop?"

The woman nodded. "I'm not law enforcement. Please do what you can to discourage other journalists from accessing our site. It's of vital importance." Her hand went up to stop Suki's next question. "I can't tell you anything. I must go now." She rose and strode away.

Mac's voice crackled in Jeff's mind. "Meet me in my office." Jeff quickly complied. It had to be something urgent. Mac began speaking as soon as Jeff entered. "Suki Kurosawa found our web address. Posing as an image recipient she got all the way through to an in-person meeting. Through the alert system I had set up, the Earth-Synon who interviewed her notified me. It's irritating that Suki wasted valuable resources, but it demonstrates a shrewd tactical mind and ability to implement plans."

Jeff was baffled that Mac had deflected his focus to this matter. He blurted out, "There have to be other reporters with the resourcefulness to get that far. Why the specific interest in her?"

Mac's eyebrows rose. "You worked with her. She's sharp and capable. Moreover, Akari showing up in Japan shows that Suki needs protection." Now, it was Jeff's eyebrows that rose questioningly, but he remained silent to allow Mac to continue. "Vera Schechner is impressed with Suki and regrets having sacked her. Also Cal Booker, one of my New York operatives, became good friends with Suki after rescuing her from Singleton's goons and setting her up in a safe house. He speaks highly of her. I'm considering bringing her on board to help us."

Jeff was shocked. "She's smart and tenacious. I'll give her that. But I'm skittish about bringing her into our small circle of humans."

"Jeff, your circle of humans is small. Mine is global. Still comparatively a select few, of course. We need all the help we can get, in myriad areas."

"Have you run this by Lew Henderson?"

"Not yet. You're the one who worked with her."

"Not that long. She's a reporter. Can we really trust her to keep such sensitive knowledge confidential? Revealing Synons would catapult her to worldwide fame and fortune."

"Vera and Cal think she has the integrity and intelligence to remain silent." He paused in thought. "I'll bring Cal on too; he can keep an eye on her—security for her and us."

"Is he human?" Mac nodded. "If they're good friends, he could have blind spots where she's concerned."

Mac shook his head. "He's from a family of Synon supporters. He's risked his life more than once for us. I trust him totally, even if he's emotionally involved with Suki. In fact, that could be a positive. If they can talk freely, he can tell her his family stories that illustrate our mission. It will bolster her loyalty."

Jeff's skepticism was visible. "Or give her a trove of material to publish with the highest bidder."

"We certainly need more Uniques here." Mac sighed. "Nevertheless, Suki and Cal will be valuable assets. I'll get it started. We'll bring them here first."

■　　■　　■

Suki was elated to get a call from Cal Booker asking if he could stop by. She hurriedly tidied her tiny short-term rental, recalling the comfortable "safe house" apartment where he had sequestered and protected her. Even though they had many long talks, he had revealed little about himself, especially his work. It was surprising to hear from him after so much time.

Standing in her doorway as he had the first time they had met, he looked like a modern-day Viking with his tall form, thick red hair, and handsome smile. "Great to see you, Suki. Sorry I haven't been in touch. MacIntyre keeps me hopping."

"Totally understood. I've been hopping myself." She invited him in and offered refreshments.

"I'm fine," he said, taking a seat. "You might need a drink, however." He grinned broadly.

Suki had scarfed down almost half a bottle of wine by the time Cal finished telling her everything. She sat in shock, mind whirling.

Cal watched her with concern. "Suki, just sit a minute. I'm gonna make coffee." He strode over to the kitchenette. She nodded, wishing she hadn't drunk the wine. More than ever in her life she needed a clear mind. She knew Cal thought a little alcohol would dull her immediate reactions, potentially fending off full-fledged shock. At least her mind hadn't gone blank in rejection of what she'd heard. She forced herself to think back to when she first met Jeff McCarthy, whom she now knew was Jeff Hawke, a human telepath who had transmitted the image received by other telepaths. The little girl, Emma, they had teamed up to find, was also a telepath.

The most shocking element was the existence of otherworldly beings posing as humans. She had met at least one! Suki shuddered recalling Akari. Had Singleton sent her? How was he involved with these Synons? Her mind began to clear. She now understood the projected image and why it was so urgent for authentic recipients to contact the Earth-Synons. Now she would be joining these "Uniques" and Synons in their mountain facility.

Since arriving back in New York, she hadn't reached out to the press about the website; now it had to be her first action. The most direct route was YCN.

Cal returned with the coffee. "Drink," he ordered.

She took control. "I need to get the word out to the press not to interfere with the website."

Cal nodded. "Yes. I've been informed that Vera Schechner is aware of everything. She's been close friends with Mac for decades and knows what he is. You can talk to her." He handed her his phone. "Here. It's secure. Do you have her number?"

"Yes." She punched it in, hoping Vera would pick-up.

■   ■   ■

Vera Schechner knew her illogical thoughts were driven by jumbled emotions. On one hand, she recognized that Suki Kurosawa was a first-rate reporter, despite sometimes skidding too close to ethical cliffs. Empathetic and insightful, she was able to connect with all types of people and would be a valuable addition to Bailey MacIntyre's team.

Yet, Vera fought her own feeling of being on the outside. Her rational mind told her that it was necessary because of her position that carried with it tremendous obligation, responsibility, and yes, influence. She could be of enormous use here doing her job. She knew that the crux of these roiling feelings was her attachment to Mac—who was not even human. Bittersweet wistfulness swept through her. She was envious of the close proximity Suki would have to Mac. An unwelcome thought appeared: was Suki a Unique? Probably not. Vera knew Mac came into contact with many people, including Uniques. She had to reconcile their vast differences with their long friendship and all that it meant.

CHAPTER TWELVE

TuMa'Aye Gra'Vay thought she had strolled from the back porch of the Dream Catcher toward the backyard pond as Tami Graves, but she had abruptly appeared in her natural energy form drifting over a barren landscape with no sign of the inn or the other buildings lining its quaint, tree-lined street. She was immediately overwhelmed by searing heat, cracked, dry soil, lack of vegetation and animals, an almost total absence of water, and a relentless sun scorching through a colorless sky.

Synons didn't perceive time like humans; those who lived on Earth learned to synchronize with the manner in which people experienced its flow. Like humans, they could not travel to the past or the future. Yet, TuMa'Aye was certain that she was being shown the future that the ecosystem surrounding the Dream Catcher could become.

Then in another sudden change, she seemed to awaken surrounded by lush tall grasses, towering unfamiliar trees, bushes, and colorful, fragrant flowers bordering a sparkling, expansive lake. The songs of birds filled the clear air. A variety of insects and small animals buzzed and scurried around her. Her mind brushed those of curious larger mammals, but no people. This and the size of the plants led her to believe she had entered a distant pre-human period of flourishing life.

A new shift now left TuMa'Aye in a familiar environment and her first glimpse of people. She floated in a dense forest looking out at a relatively large lake fed by a spring where dark-haired women were drawing water, their children laughing and frolicking in the small stream that led away from the lake. Just beyond stood a thriving Native American village. TuMa'Aye smiled wistfully. In Earth's lifespan this was the recent past, yet these people had been driven from their land.

Were these visions? Or was she actually being transported through time? The purpose was clearly for her to experience and contrast past and future in conjunction with her knowledge of the present. How was it accomplished? Did Earth possess such a remarkable ability? Or was the situation so apocalyptic that The Living World had taken this extraordinary step? TuMa'Aye burrowed into the topsoil sending her mind downward. She found a serenity unlike any she had sensed from Earth for a very long time. Sadness shook her. The serenity would soon begin its gradual decline as a new kind of human overtook this land. One that saw Earth and her resources merely as plunder for their own benefit. This bygone atmosphere told her that she had, indeed, traveled in time. She had no indication of how long she had been absent from the present.

TuMa'Aye gathered her being and floated to the treetops where she expanded her mind, asking The Living World for guidance.

■　　■　　■

The crisis of Jeff's transmission had deflected Synon attention from the search for TuMa'Aye Gra'Vay, but Tork persisted. His directions to Earth-Synons and those in the Realm to continue sending out search signals for her were lost to the urgency of contacting suspected Uniques. Even though Tork was confident that she could protect herself, he was increasingly distressed at the absence of any sign of TuMa'Aye. She was the strongest of their kind. He was aware that she sometimes blocked off her mind when engaging in certain missions, but in those cases he or others usually had knowledge of the mission and her general whereabouts. This time, Tami Graves had simply disappeared in sight of two people, including one who immediately notified Lewis Henderson. A powerful Synon, Henderson visited the Dream Catcher, searching its grounds and the surrounding area, returning in the dead of night to search more thoroughly in his natural form. All traces of TuMa'Aye Gra'Vay had vanished.

Now more Synons began to wonder if her disappearance was connected to the vision in some way. Synon morale sagged as they dealt with two simultaneous unprecedented situations.

■　　■　　■

TuMa'Aye Gra'Vay abruptly found herself back in the wasteland that exhibited no trace of life. Although the sun's glare was diffused by the dusty haze, its rays bore into her, sapping her power.

There was no shelter. She flung her being on the ground, burrowing into one of the tiny crevasses crisscrossing it and into the outer crust layer, where she compressed herself into a concentrated knot. Her mind reached through the mantle and the outer core, through rock and minerals, toward the inner core, so deep, dense, and hot that it had proved inaccessible for scientific study. The intricate makeup of this planetary interior was affected by— and affected—many things, including rotational rate. Then, for the first time since returning to the wasteland, TuMa'Aye sensed another consciousness, albeit faint. She pleaded to Earth for help to return to her persona's time. She spoke of the Uniques and the global efforts to marshal them to Earth's aid. As with every prior attempt she had made, there was no distinct reply. However, she experienced an immediate impulse to return to the surface. Sending gratitude, she summoned her strength and drove upward. Once again on the hardened dirt, she simply floated with an unencumbered mind, pushing away the sensory perceptions it allowed her to experience. Time did not exist.

Her meditative state was suddenly pierced. She was no longer floating above a barren world but in the space above it, gazing down at Earth's glory, surrounded by myriad stars. Her awareness expanded unbidden, incorporating the Synon populace and an extraordinary new phenomena—countless bewildered and stunned human minds. She worked to ascertain the source of this stunning image and was astonished to touch Jeff's mind.

■　　■　　■

Bandela-Jackson was convinced that the transmitted vision and the disappearance of TuMa'Aye Gra'Vay were connected. He was restless at the coastal North Carolina hideout, where all of the renegades had received the vision. Bandela-Jackson continued to monitor Synon activities, scoffing at the decisions they made. Why not just tell people that some of them were telepaths? Their rationales were weak. Now was the time to gather these so-called Uniques under Synon domination and make use of them.

He was tired of the renegades. Tired of hiding. Could he salvage the Jackson persona? So far his recent overtures had led nowhere. Perhaps he should contact Roger Singleton to find out what his vast network of spies and operatives might have

uncovered. Did he dare resurface as Dr. Gabe Jackson? No. Not in any public way that might alert the ever-present Synons who would send him back to the Realm in a stronger forcefield than the one he had escaped. If he were careful, however, he could contact Singleton. What he needed was a face-to-face meeting at which
he could probe Singleton's mind for undisclosed information.

■　　■　　■

Roger Singleton had been in a dither ever since his spy Akira's failed mission to locate Jeff McCarthy or any other of those who had been involved with the aliens in tricking him into releasing Emma Goodsen to them. It had all been a costly and risky under-taking with no reward for him. Unacceptable.

He was livid when Akira had called him with her sniveling story about how she couldn't get close to the YCN reporter Suki Kurosawa. She even asserted that this Kurosawa was not the same woman who had crashed his party and snooped around for the missing child, claiming she had video of herself at another event in a different location on the same night as his Naples, Florida party. The timestamp on the video she sent as proof could have been altered. How stupid did Akira think he was? His staff had dropped the ball on vetting her.

Now there was chatter from his sources about a mysterious vision that had been seen by many people, followed by a second message carrying contact information. He suspected the aliens were behind it. They had been foolish not to accept his offer of assistance in dealing with humans. Perhaps there was more than one group of aliens. Those he had encountered weren't especially impressive, despite their small spacecraft that they asserted was conscious. They had offered no proof to him. The most irritating thing was that they were already working with at least one human, Jeff McCarthy. Roger Singleton simmered; he despised sitting on the sidelines.

His mood lifted when a video call came in from the robotic prosthetics scientist Gabe Jackson. Maybe he had some information.

Singleton put on a smile and answered. "Hello Gabe. What's up? Were the geological people I sent you helpful?"

Offering no greeting, Jackson didn't smile. "Not really. Listen, I'm moving into an expansive phase of my confidential project. I'm not going back to the institute. In fact, I'm looking for a secure, secluded location."

Singleton jumped in. "You'll be interested in my Appalachian facility. It's as secure and secluded as you can get. It's not in any public listings. As you know, I have developed numerous robotic mechanisms myself for which I've sold patents. These are primarily designed for use in manufacturing. However, my personal, undisclosed work focuses on several advanced AI products as well. I should be able to offer you considerable assistance."

Jackson maintained a blank expression as he politely listened to Singleton's spiel. He stroked his short, white beard, appearing to be deep in thought. He nodded and spoke. "Roger, I had a feeling we might be kindred spirits of a sort." He offered a brief smile. "We need to talk more fully, but in person, in a location we are certain cannot be monitored in any way. Would it be possible for you to meet me at this facility of which you speak?"

Singleton could barely contain his glee, but maintained a neutral visage. "I'd be delighted."

CHAPTER THIRTEEN

Bandela-Jackson gathered the renegades for a major announcement. He could need their help again, so he was careful not to offend them. He repeated how proud he was of their progress and how grateful he was to them for helping him escape. He now needed to move on to another task which he would keep secret for all of their protection. There were Synons even more powerful than he was who could find information on his whereabouts in their minds.

As soon as night fell he set out on his journey, bypassing towns and cities to travel in his natural form westward from the flat coast through the Piedmont's rolling hills and beyond to the Appalachian mountains. Singleton had provided coordinates, so Bandela again became Jackson in the woods outside a town close to the road to Singleton's facility. There he bought a used car from a dealer who didn't seem at all concerned about verifying the personal information provided by the gentleman who appeared on foot when he was just opening his lot for the day.

The casually dressed Jackson greeted the man genially. "Good morning! I just did a rather foolish thing. I impulsively gave my car to a grandson I'm visiting. I just need one that I can drive home." He smiled broadly, walking around the lot inspecting the inventory.

The dealer was all too happy to make the sale, providing a temporary dealer license plate. Jackson paid cash and quickly drove off.

Singleton had not exaggerated when he said his facility was secluded and secure. The route followed narrow winding roads that steadily climbed into high granite mountains, through deciduous forests to slopes on which grew only alpine conifer. The road abruptly changed from paving to gravel; the terrain leveled onto a plateau. The horizon showcased mountain peaks in all directions. Jackson wondered how Singleton managed to get equipment and supplies to such a place. He followed the road to a building at which it dead-ended. It was a sturdy concrete bunker with a peaked metal roof and broad metal doors in its center. As he approached, the doors began slowly rising to allow him entry. Once inside, a barrier forced him to stop, and a man stepped up to his window, which Jackson lowered. "Dr. Jackson?" the man asked. Jackson nodded. "Welcome to our facility. Please pull ahead when the barrier lifts and park next to the wall. I'll meet you there and escort you to the elevator."

Elevator? Since it appeared to be a one-story building, Jackson surmised that the entire facility was underground. Secluded and secure indeed. Jackson was amazed when they exited the passenger elevator into an elegant lounge area, illuminated by what mimicked sunlight emanating from hidden ceiling fixtures. A door opened and a grinning Singleton strode out, approached, and vigorously shook Jackson's hand. Jackson did not like having his persona touched. He withdrew his hand as rapidly as he could while verbally greeting Singleton.

"I knew you'd be amazed," Singleton boasted as he led Jackson into his private office. "You'll be given a tour later. I'm so eager to talk to you." He motioned to a sleek lounge chair into which Jackson seated himself.

The office was spacious with the same lighting as the reception area. The wall behind him, facing Singleton's glass-topped desk, appeared to be a screen on which was displayed a scene of the surrounding mountains, giving the appearance of a window. Singleton ordered refreshments to be brought and settled into his own custom chair. "This office is secure. We can speak freely. I sense that we both find that those in charge of governments and the scientific community are less than efficient and certainly not to be trusted."

Jackson nodded. The refreshments arrived. He despised performing the motions of eating and drinking in the presence of humans, so had only asked for herbal tea, something he could easily transform into energy. Apparently, Singleton thought that a good host should always offer delicacies as well, so Jackson nibbled at a pastry, hoping the copious amount of sugar it contained wouldn't have a detrimental effect. His first encounter with such food had inadvertently caused his persona to emit a short burst of light that his human companions thankfully didn't notice, since they were busy jabbering and laughing.

Jackson dropped the pastry onto the plate in order to reply. "I'm quite concerned about certain recent occurrences. I've been able to glean very little about them. Perhaps you've had more success." He left the topic open.

Singleton's eyes narrowed. "My extensive network of reliable and discrete sources has been unsuccessful in answering my questions. Beyond our initial discussion about alarming reports of irregularities in the Earth's axial rotation, there are new reports of bizarre mass hysteria events." He paused. "You know about this?"

Jackson knew everything about the topic. He had to take care not to reveal too much. "I've heard that a message was conveyed directly to the minds of perhaps thousands of people." He noticed Singleton take on an eager expression. How much did he really know? He tried probing Singleton's mind to find it cluttered with a plethora of compartments that were surprisingly hard to penetrate. He started delicately prying them open.

Jackson continued. "It's interesting that your sources suggest mass hysteria. What is of concern is that it apparently affected people globally, not just in one location. Are you aware of any experiments that touch on this possibility?"

Singleton steepled his hands, peering at Jackson. "Do I have your word that what I reveal will be held in strictest secrecy?"

"Of course. I ask the same of you." A compartment in Singleton's mind suddenly activated; Jackon discovered that it was filled with shallow and erroneous data. For a man so obviously intelligent, Singleton was not an analytical thinker beyond technical matters.

The eager look returned to Singleton's eyes. "Definitely. I agree that these events point to a kind of mass telepathy, whether electronic or by other means. It's also of note that not everyone appears to have received it. That indicates that certain individuals were receptive while others were not. Were those who did receive it preconditioned? If so, how?"

"Do you have any ideas?" Jackson was mulling over an idea but wanted to hear what Singleton offered first. "I'm not fatigued. I'm eager to see your facility now. Is it secure to talk while we do so?"

Singleton beamed. "Of course. The entire facility is shielded and is almost totally automated. There are very few people on site at any given time. I'm able to monitor experiments and procedures remotely." He saw that Jackson was rising from his chair. "Wait a few more moments, please. I want to tell you about my most ambitious work before you see our operation."

Jackson resumed his seat, nodding. Curious, he recognized that Singleton was a genius, although one who was driven by narcissism, greed, and poor judgment.

Singleton began to pontificate. "Too many unusual things are happening with the Earth. They're trying to pass it off as caused by human activity such as deforestation, development, and burning fossil fuels. I've spent a lifetime monitoring alien activity. I am certain that it is pervasive and that extraterrestrials are behind these unprecedented natural occurrences. You are the only person so far to whom I've revealed this. I met an extraterrestrial and saw its craft."

Jackson aligned his expression to shock but said nothing.

Singleton continued, "It was a small craft for use in our atmosphere and was totally conscious. Conscious! In touch with the mothership, other craft, and the aliens." He paused, expecting to witness astonishment.

Instead, Jackson merely nodded and spoke calmly. "This is not surprising to me."

Singleton remained silent, waiting for Jackson to elaborate but was met with silence. He swiftly covered what he knew was a disappointed expression. "I expected that someone of your stature and intellect might also have excellent information sources. I offered my services to the aliens as an intermediary with the human race. Their lack of interest was a bit alarming.

It reinforced my intuition that their intentions are hostile. They have no interest in working with humans because they plan to subjugate or eradicate us. This knowledge spurred me to intensify my life work, not the robotics for which I'm famous but another application entirely. My objective is to develop a means of transferring my living mind into the protective casing of a cyborg in order to survive on a planet that becomes uninhabitable and dominated by aliens." He stopped and looked at Jackson for a reaction.

Jackson hid his astonishment and clapped his hands together. "I knew you were a visionary genius, Roger. The robotic body should be easy for you. By the way, I'm happy to offer any suggestions I can—since the connection of robotic prosthetics to the brain and nervous system is my specialty." Humans would call Singleton's revelation a stroke of luck. Due to rapid climate change and ecosystem decline, Jackson saw little hope for biological life to continue on Earth for any length of time, probably not another century. When that happened, the Realm and its inhabitants would dissolve. His objective in researching human technology had been the same as Singleton's, only his need was to fit his expansive mind into a protective, mobile body. He had no need for cumbersome neurological connections.

Singleton was effusive. "Yes! I would welcome your input. In fact, we could form a kind of partnership."

Jackson couldn't appear too eager. He also needed to leave himself free to pursue an alliance with humans and attempt a reconciliation with the Realm. "A delightful notion, but in the near future I would be unable to devote enough time and attention to it. Let's leave it loose for a while. Tell me more. I'm curious about the living brain transfer. I know others have been working on this with little progress. It seems a mammoth project."

"Not with your expertise in nerve connections."

"Aha. I see your point. Have you any experts working on this already?"

"I've found no one as yet."

Jackson nodded. "Not surprising." He pivoted to a new topic. "Roger, I appreciate your trust. I must confess a conflict of interest. Please don't be alarmed. If you partake of alcoholic spirits, now might be a time to avail yourself of a drink."

Singleton blanched. Despite Jackson's assurance, he was clearly alarmed. He turned to a cabinet behind him and retrieved a tray containing a bottle of brandy and several glasses. "Care for a brandy?" he managed a weak smile.

"Thank you, no. I can't metabolize it. You go ahead." He watched Singleton pour a glass full and gulp it down.

Singleton set the glass down and looked at Jackson. "Go ahead. I'm ready for whatever you have to tell me." He looked terrified. Did he suspect what he was about to hear?

An idea had coalesced in Jackson's mind. Did he dare take this step? He knew he was opening the figurative Pandora's box but was confident he could control what Singleton knew and, through mind control, see that he did not share it.

"Are there cameras and microphones in this room?" Jackson demanded.

"Singleton opened a panel on his desk and pressed buttons. "For my protection. I permanently destroy the recordings when I exit. They're now offline." He visibly swallowed.

"I'm aware of your surveillance of extraterrestrial activity and your encounter with the aliens. You've probably guessed. I am one myself."

Jackson was surprised at Singleton's reaction. His fear disappeared and he broke out in a wide grin. "I suspected! This is wonderful news. How can I be of service to you?"

"I'm relieved that you aren't afraid of me. Please be assured that at this time we have no extermination plans. We are merely studying you and your planet. However, that is all I can tell you. I'm prohibited from revealing where we're from, what our natural form is, and any other details about us. This is not a matter of free will on my part."

Singleton nodded vigorously. "I understand. That's a relief. I'm still hopeful that I can be of service to you."

"We need your resource network to focus on human actions and reactions to what you must now realize was our experiment. We transmitted that image to ascertain whether humans possess telepathy. We learned that some, not all, were receptive. Now we need to identify those who displayed this trait. This is a promising outcome that shows us that your species has positive potential."

Singleton looked hopeful. "Do you think we all might have telepathy but just don't access it?" Obviously, he had not received the image.

Jackson needed to string him along. This was a topic of great concern to the Synons, but it could take some time to resolve. "We think so. The history of our own species suggests it. The sooner we can begin working with these telepaths, the quicker we can learn how it is they are open to telepathy while others are not. It could simply be chemicals, genetics, or even personality traits."

Singleton perked up. "Encouraging. I will get right on it. By the way, my information network is primarily technological. Those people who work on confidential projects are proven loyalists."

"Excellent. Now let's have that tour. Is it possible for me to finish and depart before nightfall?"

"I had hoped to share my hospitality with you, but if you must depart, we'll ensure that you do. I'll have someone lead you down the mountain."

As they stood and shook hands, Jackson embedded a link in Singleton's mind, enabling him to invade it at will.

CHAPTER FOURTEEN

TuMa'Aye Gra'Vay abruptly hovered over the pond behind the Dream Catcher. She was back! She rapidly assumed her Tami Graves persona, but instead of going toward the inn she moved back into the trees. She couldn't simply reappear. She had no idea how long she had actually been gone. There was no rational explanation she could give to her human friends. Tami began trudging along the backyards behind which the stand of trees stretched for some way.

■　■　■

Lewis Henderson remained at the Native American Cultural Center. He had been busy ensuring that everything could be handled if he needed to be gone for a long time. It was past time to return to the Tech Center and provide whatever help he could. He was taking inventory in the upstairs room that held historic and significant artifacts. A presence touched his mind at the same time that Tami Graves appeared before him.

"Tami! Where the hell have you been?" Lew rushed to embrace the persona to whom he was so accustomed. She warmly returned the hug.

"I have a fantastic story but want to tell it as few times as possible. Can we go to the Tech Center?"

"Gonna make me wait, huh?" His face crinkled with a broad grin. "I'm just about done with my work here. Can you wait an hour or so for me to tie everything up?"

She grimaced. "I'm also itching to tell my adventure to everyone." She returned his grin. "Go ahead. See that this room is off limits while I get some necessary Synon sleep." Her figure began shimmering as she initiated the change to her natural state.

"You got it. I'll touch your mind when I'm ready. No need for anyone to know you're here."

There was a network of available Passageways between their Research Triangle location and the Tech Center in the mountains to the southwest. The journey took little time.

As they emerged from what they calculated to be the next to last Passageway, Tami suggested they alert Mac to their impending arrival.

■　■　■

Night had fallen and the kids had already retreated to their rooms after a long day of training. Lana Adams had pulled "babysitting" duty and was snuggled in the dormitory gathering room with a snack and a book. The other human team members, including Marie, were finishing off tasks at their workstations. As they often did, Mac and Jeff relaxed in the center's lounge, talking.

Tami's mental arrival was so strong that Jeff and Mac looked at each other in astonishment, then fired questions. Her voice took on authority. "One at a time! I'm with Lew nearby. The four of us must talk. The others can't know I'm there until we devise a plausible story. Where should we appear?"

As soon as Mac told her where he and Jeff were, the link broke. "They'll be here in a few minutes," he drawled with a smile.

■　■　■

Despite their extensive Synon lives, neither Mac nor Lew could recall an experience similar to what Tami-TuMa'Aye recounted. Jeff sat gaping in amazement at her tale.

Mac broke the silence. "The key is Earth—or whoever engineered your journey—shared Jeff's image with you, then sent you back. That seems to be a significant message."

Tami answered, "As soon as I perceived the image, my mind was invaded by countless bewildered, stunned human minds. It took all my strength to sequester them and trace the image to Jeff." She abruptly changed the subject. "Are the other Synons here?"

Mac replied, "Annilu, but we're not including her in decision-making. Judilay's still in the Bahamas; he's working with the teams trying to contact recipients." As was Mac's habit, he sat in thought for some time. The others remained silent. When he spoke again his words were measured. "Jeff, don't take this wrong, but you did seem to lack control when sending that image." Jeff grimaced. Mac continued, "In light of Tami's story, we now must entertain the thought that your action was directed."

Jeff blurted out, "I'm the only human here, so forgive me if I am offensive in any way. Is it possible that these events were initiated beyond Earth—by The Living World?"

Tami jumped in to answer. "We must consider that possibility."

"Has it done anything like this before?"

Tami responded. "We have no confirmation, yet there have been a few instances when such a possibility was considered. This is not the first time that Earth and her life have been threatened with destruction."

Lew had sat silently in thought as he listened. His human imitation of a loud intake of breath turned all attention to him as he spoke. "TuMa'Aye Gra'Vay's and Jeff's experiences are reminiscent of global indigenous stories, some told as sacred episodes, others as legends and myths. All entail a journey of self-discovery that links to the spiritual and all of Creation. As far as I know, Synons have not been privileged to share them."

■   ■   ■

When told that Suki and Cal would be joining their group, the camp Uniques were irritated that yet more regular people would be arriving.

"Why don't they bring in more people like us?" Emma demanded.

Tina and Rick chimed in simultaneous agreement then fell silent.

After a few minutes of thought, Tina remarked, "Maybe these new folk can work on getting them here."

Rick nodded. "It should be easier with adults. Our parents still don't know what we are and what's going on. At the end of summer they'll expect us to go home and back to our old lives."

"We can never do that!" Emma exclaimed. "I think my parents suspect something out of the ordinary with me. They've been through a lot, where your families haven't."

Rick scowled. "Mine was sort of suspicious. I've been careful not to let my difference show in any way. I hope Mr. MacIntyre and the group here have plans for the fall, and to get more Uniques in training."

■   ■   ■

Tami lashed out at Mac. "A reporter! How could you make such a risky decision? It's bad enough to tell her everything, but to bring her into our small circle?"

Mac remained stoic. "Isn't it better to have her close where we can observe her? If left on her own to snoop in ignorance she could do irreparable harm. Why not take advantage of her capabilities in working with us? We can use her and Cal Booker's help."

"So what do you plan on assigning them to do?" Tami demanded.

"How about what she's best at? Communications. Cal will keep an eye on her."

Jeff interjected. "I just hope the Tech Team doesn't resent her, especially if she's given a responsible assignment. The kids are already grumbling, and I have to agree with them. We must recruit Uniques that can quickly become trainers. We need them on every populated continent."

Mac's eyebrows met. "I know. I know. You both have valid points. Let's hope that the teams contacting the image recipients can begin finding recruits." He sighed. "This all happened too soon. We don't have infrastructure in place to take advantage of it."

Lew lifted the mood. "When did you borrow Jeff's noisy sighing?"

"When did you?" Mac retorted. Everybody laughed.

Jeff quipped, "I guess it's contagious."

"It's late," Tami observed. "Jeff needs his sleep and we need rest. Let's reconvene early tomorrow. We have to plan what to tell the kids and the Tech Team about my journey."

Jeff had grown bolder. "I want to tell them everything and keep them apprised of everything that's going on. They've more than proven their loyalty and worth." He paused. "And that goes for Annilu as well. Judilay is already assuming responsibility."

Tami replied, "Agreed. The Bandela data project is almost done. We need to pivot the team to our larger enterprise, if they want it. As for Annilu, well, she's still green as an Earth-Synon, but strong and dedicated. We must give them all every opportunity."

Mac sat with steepled fingers. "Agreed."

■　　■　　■

Suki Kurosawa was glad that she had no lease to break. What household furnishings she had not sold or donated were safely in storage, awaiting the permanent home that now looked farther in the future. She was excited and a bit anxious about what that future would bring for her. She hoped she could gain trust and prove herself worthy of it.

She contacted a few close friends and relatives to tell them she had a new assignment that could put her out of touch for a while, reassuring them that she would be in no danger, simply traveling and kept busy.

She wasn't surprised that a private plane had been arranged for their move, flying between private airports. Having Cal along was the proverbial icing on the cake. In addition to their personal belongings, the flight was taking supplies to the Camp, so they had a spacious cabin to themselves, complete with a small refreshment area. They relaxed and chatted, exchanging stories. She was still somewhat in a state of disbelief, and Cal tried to explain more to her about the Synons and his family's long tradition of aiding them. He helped her connect the dots in her experience working with Jeff in Florida to locate Emma Goodsen.

"Even though Roger Singleton is a scary guy, I want to know more about him," she admitted. "Why did he fixate on finding me?" She shivered, recalling her encounter with him.

Cal replied, "He thinks you can lead him to the extraterrestrials he wants to cozy up to. He seems capable of doing whatever is necessary to achieve his goal. I mean, he even kidnapped a child because he thought she was in touch with them! He's dangerous. But you'll be protected from him."

Suki mused, "Vera was researching him. I wonder if she's found anything more. He seems to be into a lot of things."

"Mac was looking into him too. His high security clearance and network will eventually lead him to answers."

Suki was skeptical. "Singleton hasn't been brought to justice for the kidnapping and imprisonment of a child. He probably thinks he can get away with anything."

"He doesn't know what he's up against." Cal chuckled. "You could lead him to extraterrestrials, just not the kind he thinks."

The pilot's voice interrupted. "We're starting our descent. Buckle up."

■　　■　　■

As they glided to a stop, Suki saw Jeff and two other men standing on the tarmac. Behind them were a pickup and a large box truck. In the near distance, she saw that they were ringed by mountains.

When they started down the gangplank, Jeff warmly greeted them. "Welcome to North Carolina, it's a bit of a drive to the camp, so you can take in the scenery." He led them toward the pickup. "My truck cab can easily fit the three of us. We'll get your luggage secured in the bed. The other truck is for the supplies and equipment. We're glad to get it."

Suki felt comforted sitting between Jeff and Cal in the truck. His last name was different, but Jeff was the same guy she had gotten to know and trust in Florida. He chattered as they rode along curvy wooded roads in which a few late summer flowers still bloomed despite some leaves beginning to turn. At times she caught her breath as they rounded a curve to a stunning vista.

Cal exclaimed, "I'm gonna love it here!"

The camp and Tech Center were situated off a couple of winding, steep two-lane roads. As they approached a squat brick building perched next to a river, Jeff began his tour speech. "That's the Tech Center. The reason we're located here."

Suki blurted, "It's sure isolated; how do you get in and out in bad weather?"

Jeff chortled. "That's the point. Hard to find. We've been here over a year and no strangers have ever stumbled upon us. Bad weather is one of the reasons we make sure we stay well-supplied. We have solar panels and a water-powered generator. There's a small dam just out of sight."

Cal remarked. "I assume Mac found this spot."

"Of course," Jeff replied with a grin. "If we went on along the road a bit we'd see the quarters for our people. An old motel that the Synons refurbished. Each of the single people has a small apartment. Marie and I share a cabin on a bend in this river just a ways on. We have a small, vetted maintenance staff. Several of them live in the motel and some have houses nearby. The Synons live in a big old farmhouse in this direction, between the Tech Center and the camp. That's where we're going." Suki and Cal listened carefully as he continued. "When you see it, you'll be amazed that the camp actually was a dilapidated old summer camp."

Jeff turned onto a narrow gravel road that was barely visible within the trees. "Sorry about the bumpy ride. We'll pave this eventually." They drove through the forest to a partial clearing. "We left as much natural vegetation as we could. I love the way the cabins are nestled within it."

Suki was surprised. "This is so cute! It looks like a little fairy village."

"Or maybe a gnome village," Cal drawled.

Various sized wood and stone structures were interspersed at angles within trees, bushes, flowers, grass, and pathways. Their peaked roofs lent quaintness.

"The Synons need Nature," Jeff explained. "They use its energy to help maintain their personas."

"That's just amazing," Suki murmured. She was nervous about meeting them.

Jeff pulled to a stop in front of a building bisected by a screened enclosure. "Here's home sweet home," Jeff said, opening his door. Cal followed his cue to exit, then helped Suki navigate the step down to the ground. Jeff was unloading their luggage. Before moving to help him, Suki had to glance at the cottage that was stone on the lower half with wood above.

"Can one of you latch the screened door open?" Jeff said, approaching with a bag in each hand. Cal bounded up the two short steps in one stride and followed the instructions. "Nice!" he said.

When she entered, Suki saw that the screened enclosure was like a breezeway between two sections of the building. Each had windows and a door opening onto it. She asked, "Are both sides the same?"

"Yep," Jeff said. "Take whichever one you want. Hope you don't mind sharing a porch; this was built for teachers. You each have a little apartment with a kitchenette. We actually have many of our meals together in the gathering hall. Whose bag is this?" He pointed to a wheeled suitcase.

"Mine," Suki said.

"Does which side matter?"

"Oh, no," she replied, anxious to see inside.

Jeff opened the door and slid the case in. "Do we have everything off the truck?" he asked.

Cal was already taking his stuff into the other apartment. "Yeah."

Suki took that as an invitation to enter her new home. It was tiny but cozy and inviting. The front half was a living room with a desk, television, and sofa. On the far wall she saw a small kitchen area. She followed Jeff as he took her luggage through a door to the bedroom on the back of the structure. "Oh, I love it!" She ran to the back wall where French doors opened onto a small deck with a railing from which trailed flowers.

Jeff said, "Okay. The others are waiting. We better get going."

■ ■ ■

At the end of the road sat the biggest building, ringed with large windows and decks. "That's the gathering hall," Jeff said, pulling onto a mulched parking area.

They entered what looked to Suki like the lobby of a rustic hotel. It was dominated by a large stone fireplace around which were arrayed sofas, chairs, and tables. with one smaller sofa occupied by three children, one of whom she recognized as Emma Goodsen. Emma smiled at her. Relief—the child appeared not to despise her.

Suki's eyes swept over the adults nearly equally divided between people of both primary genders. Which ones were the Synons? She felt a mixture of awe, excitement, and anxiety.

One of two older men jumped up and greeted Cal, then turned and grabbed her hand. She felt warmth and strength—and mass; the feeling of a human hand. "Suki, welcome. We're thrilled to have you and Cal join us. I'm Bailey MacIntyre."

Bailey MacIntyre! What looked like an aging baby-boomer with shoulder-length gray hair, bushy eyebrows, and a fit body was not a human at all! As she understood it, this was a bundle of energy somehow taking on not only the appearance but the volume and mass of a flesh and blood person. Realizing she was staring at him, Suki felt her face flush. She looked down.

MacIntyre guffawed. "You have much better self-control than most people do when first meeting one of us." Suki managed a half smile. He kept talking. "Might as well introduce you to the rest of us so you can relax." As she met Annilu, Lewis Henderson, and Tami Graves, Suki recalled Cal's tidbits about each, removing some of their strangeness. She realized that she could have identified each of them by their appearance and body language, or in Annilu's case, lack of it. Suki's tension began draining away.

The human Tech Team members were delightful as well. She would enjoy working and living among them. The three children sat silently watching as she was introduced to the adults. As MacIntyre turned to the children, Emma spoke. "Hello Miss Kurosawa. It will be good to have you with us."

By the time she finally was coaxed into an easy chair and a glass of wine placed in her hand, Suki was smiling with genuine joy. How lucky she was!

CHAPTER FIFTEEN

Now comfortable once again in his Gabe Jackson persona, Bandela kept mental tabs on Roger Singleton. The prompt Bandela had planted in the eccentric inventor's mind was stimulating him to design a kind of robot he had not yet attempted—a cyborg that would look like a human, with the same types of mobility. Jackson tweaked the prompt to reduce Singleton's obsession with a machine that could replace his own body and encase his brain to one that could be produced more quickly. Jackson only wanted a secure, durable, casing for his own essence. Mobility and dexterity were crucial, of course, but given the erratic and weakening condition of the Earth, the speed at which a workable model could be available was the most vital aspect.

At present, only the most sensitive and advanced geological sensors were detecting minute alterations in the rate at which the planet rotated on its axis. However, Jackson was convinced that he could harness the power of the Synon link with the Earth for a far more accurate reading; what he found was much more alarming. The scientific community knew what would happen if it worsened, but they had no idea of what to do to prevent it. This could be a more immediate catastrophe than the cumulative effects of climate change.

Since leaving Singleton's facility, Jackson had remained in the mountains, moving in his natural form through the wildest areas. The plant and animal life was tense, as if aware that dangerous upheavals could be imminent. Each time he attempted to access what he now accepted was Earth's consciousness, he confronted the same feeble message: they must help.

An inner struggle seized his mind. How could he assist his fellow Synons, to whom Earth obviously referred, without being imprisoned again? He knew that a number of them were nearby; he was using a great deal of his power blocking out their mental buzz. There was no way he could contact any one of them without being recognized. These were some of the very Earth-dwellers who had supported TuMa'Aye Gra'Vay the night he was defeated as Bandela. For him at the moment, the danger she and her cohorts posed outweighed the Earth's need. However, given the planet's condition, its life and that of the Realm, including him, could soon be faced with extinction. He was faced with the kind of dilemma to which he was unaccustomed.

Drifting down the slope of a ridgeline, Bandela-Jackson gradually descended from alpine to more diverse tree and ground cover. He had moved quite a distance from Singleton's facility and needed to find a suitable spot for a short respite.

■　　■　　■

Earth-Synons had developed psychic tendrils of sensory perception that persisted when they dropped their personas and returned to their essential form. Now as Bandela slipped into the Synon sleep state, he felt the atmosphere change. The cool breeze bearing mingled forest scents vanished, replaced by blasts of frigid air. Bringing himself to full awareness, Bandela now wore his old default persona of a short, portly man with a porcine face.

Irritated and confused, he wondered why. Like other longtime Earth-Synons, Bandela had generated rudimentary emotions; he especially developed the feelings of resentment, rage, and other negative passions that drove his mindset and actions. A palpable terror now overtook him, as he became aware of the environment surrounding him.

In all directions lay ice striated by dirty cracks. A dim gray sky surrounded the area like a lid. Bandela started walking, looking for any variation in the landscape. When he found it, he was nearly swept over the edge of the glacier that he traversed. His feet stood in puddles from which ran streams of water splashing over the side. He looked down to a turbulent sea below, encircled by high, jagged glaciers from which melting water poured. Bandela's magnetic sense told him that he was in the polar Arctic. Was he experiencing reality or a hallucination? If reality, how had he come to be here?

The landscape shifted under Bandela and he toppled over the precipice. He managed to regain his essential form midair. As he slammed into water, Bandela was only a loose conglomeration of energy that shot downward. Calling on all his power, he forced himself back to the surface to find he was no longer in the Arctic. Waves surged. The sky was a sickly yellow. He was unable to pull himself above the roiling water, but he succeeded in compressing his essence into a small mass with sufficient buoyancy to stay afloat.

He summoned his sensory perception. The water was so hot that it must be on the verge of boiling. Could anything be alive within its depths? He visually surveyed the surroundings. Dark ocean water churned to the horizon on three sides. The fourth was so astounding that he doubted the efficacy of his perception. In the distance, the distinct skyline of a city rose from the watery expanse. But only the upper parts of the tallest buildings were visible. The city had been inundated by the sea. Where was he? When was he? Pieces clicked into place. He had become part of the process in which global warming was melting arctic ice that warmed and raised the oceans, overtaking global shorelines and relentlessly advancing inland. It seemed like a crude child's fable. If his Bandela personality had been in charge, he would have sneered at its simplistic message and delivery method. Was Earth the storyteller? Was it—or "she" as so many preferred to say—attempting to propel him to action? His innate Synon intellect emerged. Perhaps he had been transported to the near future. Was he being tasked to raise a warning by this planet to which his kind was interconnected to the point that if its life vanished the Synons would also?

■　　■　　■

Abruptly, Bandela stood beneath the mountain canopy. Irritated, he awkwardly transitioned to his Jackson persona. He felt an unnatural need for companionship. Was there a small town nearby where Jackson was unknown and could at least stroll along its main street soaking up its vapid normalcy?

Opening a sliver of his mind, he cast outward for human activity but was overwhelmed by a strong Synon presence. Using the techniques learned from his former renegade companion Bret, he bolstered his mental block while extending a strand of awareness to the strongest mind. His block almost dropped at the shocked recognition that it was TuMa'Aye Gra'Vay.

■　　■　　■

At the camp, a welcoming party was organized for Suki, Cal, and Tami. It provided an opportunity for everyone to gather in the forest bordering the camp for refreshments, relaxation, and conversation. As soon as Tami appeared, Emma Goodsen threw her arms around her as if she were any other person. Tami returned the embrace. "I'm so glad to see you, Emma!"

Tami mingled, trying to spend a few minutes with each attendee, paying special attention to the two new Unique children.

At length, Mac called the group to attention. "Can everyone get comfortably seated? Tami has a story you must hear. Please hold questions and comments until she has finished."

Tami moved to the center of the group. "You might well be the only people who will ever know about my recent experience. I trust all of you and know you will understand the importance of keeping it confidential."

As Tami spoke, her audience sat mesmerized. When she finished, Tami glided to her chair and sat. "As I spoke, it seemed that I was reliving each moment," she murmured. "Let's take a short break before we discuss it."

Emma rushed to take Tami a glass of iced tea. "Do you need anything else?" she asked anxiously.

Tami smiled affectionately at the girl. "Thank you, darling. I'll be fine."

A few others silently strolled around the area, refreshing their glasses. All were deeply affected.

Marie and Jeff sat on a bench holding hands. As Tami spoke, she had stolen looks at Jeff; he sat in rapt attention.

Tami stood. "Now I'll try to answer—" Her countenance hardened as she looked to her fellow Synons, all of whom had risen to an alert position. "Bandela!" She spat out the word.

Lew, Mac, and Annilu were running toward the forest. The startled humans had also stood, wearing alarmed expressions.

"Jeff," Tami spoke rapidly. "Take everyone to the Tech Center's secure space right now, even though I sensed no Synons other than Bandela. Stay until you hear from one of us." As she ran toward the forest, her figure began to shimmer and waver.

The Tech Team were well acquainted with Bandela, having spent the prior year sifting through the reams of data Bandela had infested a municipal computer network with. It had been transmitted to the team by the high security scientists who were examining pages handed to them through a slot in his protective Faraday cage by Josh Jackson, the persona they had changed Bandela into, fabricating him as a human hacker who had invaded and altered the network's entire coding and software structures. The team received data that could possibly rebuild that system, enhancing its capacity and capabilities in the process, however, extreme care was required to prevent the possibility of unknown viruses that could spread, endangering global communications. The Tech Team combed through what was sent to them, compiling instructions to the awaiting municipal staff.

The team had heard all the stories of Bandela's attacks and the extraordinary events that led to his being captured and imprisoned. After he completed his task on Earth as Josh, Bandela had been banished to the Realm within the energy field from which Bret's group had helped him escape.

The two new young Uniques had heard most of that story, but were unsure of what they heard Tami exclaim before instructing Jeff to whisk them away. "No time for talk!" Jeff shouted as he beckoned everyone to parked vehicles. "Kids, jump in the bed of my truck." Marie was already herding them; once they were secure, she jumped into the passenger seat and the truck lurched away. The Tech Team piled into one car and sped off right behind them.

■　■　■

As soon as Mac and Lew were out of sight they transformed. Following the others, Mac's voice roared in Annilu's mind. "Annilu, we can handle Bandela. We need you to stay with the people. You can help protect them if it comes to that, but more importantly, you'll be able to work with Jeff to communicate with us."

"Yes sir." Annilu completed her transition and floated off toward the Tech Center. She quickly blocked the other three, knowing their attention would be outward toward Bandela. She wasn't ready for them to witness the resentment seething within her. Jeff had telepathed an image around the world; he could easily communicate with three strong Synons within a few miles of his location. They just didn't want to include her. Here she was babysitting humans while Judilay was off leading a Confluence center. Judilay! He was an embarrassment! She had to control herself before arriving at the Tech Center where she must pretend to comply with her orders.

As she floated away, Annilu heard her former companions conversing.

"Any ideas?" Tami asked.

Lew responded. "Bandela's strong. He already knows exactly where we are."

Mac spoke decisively, "Come on." He headed toward Bandela's location. "We need to keep him as far away from the camp as possible."

"Roger that!" Tami quipped. Then sped northward.

CHAPTER SIXTEEN

The same three that had pursued, taunted, and defeated Bandela over a year ago were now almost upon him. A sudden urge propelled him to action. When the trio materialized, they found a thin, pale young man sitting on a log. He had a shock of unruly red hair, portions sticking straight up and others dropping over one eye. A gold earring dangled from one ear and a swipe of auburn beard crossed his chin. They surrounded him. The air crackled with energy. He stood.

"Well, well. Look who crawled out from under a log," MacIntyre drawled. "I guess you like the son we devised for Gabe Jackson."

Josh Jackson's eyes blazed. "Thought I'd try him out, since only a handful of people recognize him."

"What do you want?" Tami spat. "You must really need something to muster the nerve to meet us."

"A truce." Josh rushed on, their contempt reverberating in his mind. He peered at Tami. "I saw everything. Your journey. Jeff's image." He saw and felt their surprise. "Then Earth took me on a similar journey."

Lew Henderson snapped, "Why would Earth bother with the likes of you?"

"Since I returned I've been monitoring the rotational fluctuations. It is alarming. I tried to form a bond with—her. I guess it worked."

The three were silent. He knew they were communicating behind their formidable mental barriers. He had to work hard at maintaining the Josh persona and its dispassionate expression. He was at their mercy. What had led him to put himself in such a vulnerable position?

"Tell us your experience," Tami demanded.

Relief. They were at least giving him a chance to explain. "First, I must stress that this has changed me. The peril facing this planet can lead to our extinction. I'm convinced that Earth wants all the Synons to unite and save it—her."

"Nice speech. You can understand why we can't believe it," Mac said. "Go ahead and tell us your adventure. You were always quite the raconteur."

Josh dropped back to the log, beckoning the others to sit on others nearby. They complied. Although the three figures looked relaxed, Josh knew that each was ready to unleash a torrent of power at him in an instant. He began his tale. "My experience took me to the Arctic and the equator."

■　　■　　■

After listening attentively to Bandela's extraordinary tale, the Synon trio sat in silent communication while Josh fidgeted.

Mac was skeptical. "Dare we trust him at all?"

Lew noted, "His barrier is down. I sense no treachery."

Tami peered at the youthful figure. Instead of discussing what they had just heard, she asked her companions, "Why bring out Josh?" Then she continued without waiting for a reply. "Is he incapable of creating an original persona? Is he trying to ingratiate himself by using the one we devised?"

Mac's bushy eyebrows rose. "You think that choice has a bearing on the issue at hand?"

Tami nodded. "How strong is he on Earth without his followers?"

Josh squirmed under their scrutiny. Lew remarked, "He's uncomfortable. I think you're right. He loses his bluster without backup."

Mac was persistent. "So do we trust him? Do we believe him?" He turned his gaze from Josh to Tami.

Her eyes remained on the young man whose persona she noticed was slightly wavering. "Never trust him. He's corrupted. As for the experiences he says he had, I'm inclined to accept them. I suggest a test."

Her two companions gave her understanding looks. "Let's get to it." Mac said.

When they rose and walked toward him, Josh flinched and stood.

Tami spoke commandingly, "Josh, as a Synon, there are lines you can never cross. Nevertheless, we are acquainted with your strengths and weaknesses; we can, and will, control both." Josh nodded. It was apparent that he struggled to maintain his persona.

Mac turned, waving his arm toward the inner forest. "Let's go deeper into the woods." He led the group with Tami and Lew flanking the stumbling Josh Jackson. They reached a small clearing that was colorful with wildflowers; it was centered by two streams that met just above a bubbling spring that bounded over a rocky prominence to form one wider creek. Mac stopped and murmured. "I'm revealing to you what people would call my secret happy place."

"Thank you," Lew whispered.

"Glorious," Tami flung her arms out, twirling. "Do you like it, Josh?"

The young man smiled. "Yes. It's speaking to my true nature as a Synon."

The trio silently conferred.

"I think he might actually be telling the truth," Lew offered.

"Let's do it," Mac urged.

Tami glided toward the spring. "Earth is very accessible through water," she said, beckoning Josh to join her. Her two male friends escorted him to her side and positioned themselves so that Josh was encircled. Tami addressed Josh. "Have you talked to her since your journey?"

"Once. Briefly."

"Now's the time to offer your gratitude and ask for guidance."

A look of trepidation flitted across his face. "Here? With you watching? And listening?"

She nodded. "We'll be unintrusive. Unless you try some trick."

He sagged in resignation. "Okay, I'll try to contact Earth. I've never done it while holding a persona, though."

"You know we can't allow you to drop it," Mac retorted.

"Maybe you could drop yours? It would help me feel more like I'm alone."

Tami's voice carried it's commanding authority. "You'll still be surrounded. We can perceive the most miniscule intention or action."

"I understand. I really do want to help. If this planet becomes unlivable, so will I."

"So do it," Mac ordered, beginning to shimmer.

■　　■　　■

In moments, Josh appeared to stand alone by the spring. However, he was acutely aware of the crackling energy surrounding him and the observant tendrils it gently placed in his mind.

Josh knelt and tried to push their presence aside, directing his mind into the spring, recalling his prior engagements with the planetary consciousness. Perhaps it was a helpful nudge from the interlopers, or simply the location, but he quickly felt a new presence. This time, it didn't seem to be far away; it was right there, and everywhere. He felt a welcoming warmth engulf his being and found himself speaking aloud, as if he were really a man. "Please let me help," he wailed. He recalled Tami's instructions. "Thank you for showing me what's ahead. What can I do to stop it?"

"Follow The Living World." He flinched. He heard nothing, but it had seemed like a voice issuing orders.

"Yes. Yes. I'm going to work on that. But what can I do specifically to help my kind fix things here?"

"Only they can help."

"Yeah, I know. Us, the Synons. What do we need to do?"

"Not you. They."

"Oh no. Please give me a chance. I'll work with my kind." He sensed impatience.

"They. Nourish them."

"I should nourish my fellow Synons?"

"No. Them." Earth's presence was gone, but the ones in his head were clamoring.

■　■　■

The trio reappeared in human form just in time to catch Josh as he crumbled to the ground in exhaustion. His persona wildly fluctuated like a light rapidly being turned on and off. Still distrustful, they fed tiny amounts of power to him in a rhythmic pattern. Gradually, the figure of the young man solidified. He sat on a rock trying to get his bearings. "I assumed she needs the Synons to unite and help her, but she seems to mean someone else. Do you know what she means?"

Tami spoke aloud to her companions, "He was sequestered when we discovered Uniques."

Josh perked up. "Uniques? The humans who perceived Jeff's image?"

Tami silently conferred with Mac and Lew. "We have to tell him. He'll find out one way or another." They concurred. "Josh, we've learned that there are many humans who can communicate telepathically with one another and Synons, some with animals as well."

Josh interrupted, "I know. I've monitored the communication. Human telepathy isn't surprising. It should be an innate ability. I think they all probably have it. Throughout their history there have been reports suggesting it. Humans must have reached the evolutionary threshold for it to manifest."

Tami chortled. "We forget that you're the Realm's longtime archivist. You might be right. The vital thing now is that Earth is telling us it is they—the Uniques as we call them—who are the only ones capable of saving her and all the life she supports."

"Do they have extraordinary powers beyond telepathy?"

"We don't yet know. We're working with a few of them and reaching out to those who received the image. There's a global network of Earth-Synons working to identify and persuade them to join us for training."

"What kind of training?"

Mac interjected, "Initially, how to use and control their telepathy. We want to gather enough of them to be able to communicate with Earth for further guidance."

Josh shook his head. "I don't get it at all. What could a bunch of humans do that we can't? That's insulting!"

Mac's countenance darkened. "You appear to have learned nothing in your time here."

A hint of Bandela's bluster appeared. "Oh, I learned plenty! Just you wait 'til…" He abruptly shut up.

Mac glared at him. "Until what!"

Josh's body language mirrored Bandela's as he attempted to feign nonchalance. "Oh, just 'til you spend more time with me. I learned what they call the good, the bad, and the ugly about humans. I understand pretty well what makes them tick. And that doesn't include giving up anything now to make things better in the future. They're strictly self-serving."

Lew shook his head. "You attracted, and were attracted to, the worst of the worst. And you incorporated it into your persona. I firmly believe the majority of people are much more altruistic than you think." He lapsed into thought, then added, "Didn't you encounter caring people while doing Gabe Jackson's prosthetics work?"

Josh glowered. "Cutthroat competitiveness. A race for fame and fortune."

"You weren't touched at all when you saw how you were helping people?"

"I was in the fame and fortune game too. Those who displayed signs of empathy and caring were just out to make points with whatever power they looked to, especially those who feared punishment in the afterlife."

Tami's concerned expression spoke as loudly as her words. "How is it that a Synon can think and behave in ways so opposite to our purpose and nature? And there are others who follow him."

Josh snorted a laugh. "They were at it long before I got here. I learned from them. And people."

Tami's head dropped. "There have always been bad people. You and your gang appear to be the first bad Synons we've witnessed. I don't understand why now."

Mac mused, "Perhaps they were always here, adept at avoiding detection."

Thoughtful silence fell. Then Tami adopted a resilient posture. "Our task is Earth. Humans have developed pervasive self-interest that drives their motivations and actions. Now they're learning by experience that controlling climate change and ecosystem destruction is vital for their own comfort, at the least, and potentially their own survival and that of their species. That's a strong evolutionary imperative."

"So these Uniques are going to persuade the whole world to make sacrifices for everybody else?" He barked a laugh. "How! By controlling their minds?"

Lew looked stricken. "I truly hope not," he muttered. "That's against our—"

Josh cut him off, "Our directives. Not theirs. You don't think many of these people who suddenly discover they're telepathic won't use it for their own ends?"

The trio looked at one another. Tami said quietly, "Leave it to you to conjure up the worst of human impulses." She sighed. "I hate to admit it, but you've raised a potentiality we hadn't explored." She thought a moment. "But Earth seems to know something we don't."

CHAPTER SEVENTEEN

Lana Adams was using her education and experience in psychology to develop training criteria for Uniques. She tried to work from their perspective, addressing potential emotional responses to their new circumstances. She recalled her own shock at learning that Jeff and Emma possessed the same telepathic abilities as the otherworldly beings she had come to know at the center. It was a shock to learn that Jeff was able to astral travel and then broadcast an image to all Synons and those humans who were also telepathic.

Lana embraced the Synon concept of all Creation as The Living World. She thought it was perhaps easier for her than many people, since her background involved the study of psychology as well as spirituality ranging from traditional religions to ancient belief systems. Lana was empathetic and intuitive, giving her deep insight into others.

This morning she had remained at home to work in her comfortable studio apartment. She found it much more conducive to analysis and creative thought than the available small cubicles next to the open main Tech Center workroom.

Lana sipped her coffee as she stared out the large window at sunbeams playing on trees. She was deep in thought trying to project emotional milestones that would occur as Uniques underwent training. Her focus wandered and Judilay's face popped into her mind. She remembered that just before waking that morning she had dreamed about him interacting with people. She really missed her Synon friend.

Reacting to the abrupt jangle of her phone, Lana almost spilled her coffee. When she saw the name flashed on the screen she hastily put down the coffee and answered. "Judilay! I just thought about you!"

"Well, I'm glad to hear that! Do you have time for a video call?"

"Of course."

When his face appeared on her screen, she felt warmth flow through her. They both began speaking at once then stopped, allowing a moment of silence. "You're so happy!" she exclaimed. "I knew you'd be great working with people."

Judilay looked a bit perplexed, then grinned. "Is it that obvious? Yeah, my interactions with Uniques have been much better than I could have hoped for."

Lana felt prickly. She was having the strangest sensation. Just before Judilay spoke, she knew every word he would say. Watching him and feeling his elation and pride, she said nothing, but Judilay was aware of their mental link.

"Lana! You can hear my thoughts!" He looked about to weep.

"Yes!" Tears came to her eyes and rolled down her cheeks. "I must be a Unique!"

"This is so wonderful! It means so much!" He sobered. "But you need some guidance on controlling it. I'll give you some pointers on filtering out others and focusing your mental attention. You know, being able to block all the babble of surrounding minds is essential."

Lana thought about how vital that was to new Uniques. "I can use that," she murmured.

"Huh? Oh, yeah. Control should be the major part of the training. The kids there can help with that through their own experience."

Lana's mind was hurtling like a runaway train. "When can you come back here?" Then her face fell. "Yeah, I know. You can't. What you're doing there is too important. The kids here are clamoring for students. Isn't that a hoot? Kids demanding people of any age to teach. They're really upset about the—" She caught herself, but it was too late.

Judilay knew the next word she would have said was "hoax."

"No!" he roared. "I thought they had given up on that idea." Lana felt anger rising. Was it just her own or was Judilay's compounding it? Was he developing emotion? Of course. She had always felt it in him. She saw signs of rapid emotional responses flitting across his countenance.

"I'm sorry," she whispered. "Mac insists that too many wild stories are spreading. There are calls for investigations. We need to squelch it all immediately by putting out a story of it being an elaborate hoax begun by a few people."

"Why would anybody believe that story more than the others? We're telling the Uniques that it was a human Unique who somehow had the power to transmit an image to other Uniques around the world."

"They apparently don't think non-Uniques will understand that. They're trying to work out details on how it might have been accomplished by a group who fabricated the story, then used technology and the power of suggestion to make others believe it."

"I've been so immersed I haven't had time to follow media on it. I heard crazy stories are spreading. Sounds like the biggest one is that it was aliens."

"Yes. We thought of encouraging that, but then governments would investigate."

Judilay's face clouded. "The answer is not to tell Uniques that their ability isn't real when they know what they perceived. That will just confuse and anger them. They'll never contact us. I feel so bad for Jeff. He must be blaming himself for a colossal lapse in self-control."

Lana felt sadness tinged with lingering anger overcoming her. She couldn't help Judilay if she couldn't disentangle herself from his emotions. An image of a door slamming shut appeared; her psychic link with Judilay was cut off.

He stared at her. "What did you do?"

Tears were freely flowing down her face. "I think I willed myself to cut your mind off. I can't help you if I'm immersed in your despair." There was no need to articulate an acknowledgement of the bond they had formed. It was apparent and inevitable. She attempted a smile. "Jeff insists that he was directed to share that image by either Earth or The Living World. Tami seemed to agree, but she has no evidence. Judilay, I think he knows in his heart that it was beyond his control. There's a larger purpose to it all. You have to believe that."

He nodded. "I thought of that also, but it just seemed to me like grasping for excuses. If it's true, I wish whoever did it would give us some affirmation."

"Oh, so do I. But it just might not be the plan. You have to be strong and keep working. If the Uniques are the only ones Earth says can help her, they are priority. And you have the ability to connect with them and discover who among them has the most potential for training and conducting their eventual mission."

He looked wistful. "I wish you could come down here. We could use more help."

"I wish I could too."

. . .

Jeff wore a puzzled look. "Why didn't it show up before?"

Tami answered, "Many reasons could apply. Over time, Lana and Judilay formed a strong friendship. Perhaps their physical separation triggered her latent ability. Lana has said she's had exceptional experiences before."

Mac, Tami, Jeff, and Lana sat on the wide wraparound porch of the Synons' camp home. Lana was relieved that Lew and Annilu had taken the kids on an outing. She sensed that Annilu strongly disapproved—and was even jealous—of Lana's bond with the Synon who had initially been intended as Annilu's partner.

At the mention of the bond between Judilay and herself, Lana had noticed a fleeting glance pass between Jeff and Tami that seemed laden with content. She recalled bits of information about their initial relationship in which Jeff was infatuated with Tami. Later, after realizing what she had done, Jeff had displayed bitterness; Tami had expressed regret. Now they appeared to get along, at least as colleagues.

Lana waited for one of them to speak, but neither did. Lana decided to bring up something that occurred to her. "A metaphor came to me." The other three regarded her receptively, waiting for her to continue. "Quantum particles and entanglement."

Mac nodded. "Einstein's spooky action at a distance."

Lana laughed. "From what I understand very simply, recent experiments suggest particles that can affect each other over any distance, even across the universe."

Tami interjected. "They appear to be closely connected, to the extent that some scientists say they might be regarded as one, even though they might be far apart."

Jeff had been quietly listening. "What about living things?"

Mac's eyebrows rose. "In the quantum sense? I don't know about that. The meaning of entanglement existed long before it was applied to quantum physics. There's work on it being done in many technical fields, like computing. I think the way Lana referred to it as metaphorical in human relationships is appropriate."

Jeff stared at his hands folded in his lap and muttered. "Marie feels my bond with Cosmos is closer than ours 'cause I can mentally communicate with him and not her."

Lana reached over and touched Jeff's arm. "That's normal. If we're confessing here, the Tech Team feels like outsiders to some extent because we aren't Uniques. Well, that no longer includes me."

Tami looked stricken. "I'm so sorry. We know, and have really tried to let all of you know how much we value you, professionally and personally."

"Humankind is early in its growth," Mac said.

"Meaning you know things you can't tell us," Jeff growled.

Mac glared at him. "We need to move our focus to Lana's request to join Judilay in the Bahamas. We must consider priorities in every decision we make. Training Uniques as quickly as possible is paramount. Lana, your work will be vital in helping us and them. I want nothing to interfere with it."

Lana smoldered. "What if my relationship with Judilay—"

It was Mac's turn to explode. "Relationships cannot impede our mission! There will be a time to further explore links between humans and Synons. You are a Unique. We need you here to continue your psychological checklist, but also to begin training. We need you asap to train other adults who might balk at having child instructors."

Jeff addressed Mac quietly, "It won't be easy for her." Then his attention turned to Lana. "I hate to be so blunt, but it must be said. You're a female human who might, just might, have become emotionally attached to a Synon male persona in the way you would a man. That's fraught with implications."

Lana's felt her face grow hot and hoped her dark skin would hide the blush blooming on her cheeks. "I'm aware of that. I'd like to know how other Earth-Synons have dealt with it."

Mac looked pained. "Synons don't have emotions like people." He paused. "At least that's always been the case. We have a kind of empathy and caring, and we've learned to mimic human body language to convey the impression of feelings, but we don't have the emotional reactions generated by Earth biology."

"What if we're evolving?" Tami whispered.

Mac's lips pursed, illustrating the point he had just made. "It's true that the advent of digital knowledge has enabled Earth-Synons to learn how the human body functions and incorporate that knowledge into their personas' behavior. I've no doubt that some are dabbling with constructing semblances of chemical and neurological systems." He looked pointedly at Tami. "Those of us who've been here, interacting with people, have intrinsically adapted our personas to enhance those interactions in the service of our mission."

Lana found Mac's attitude cold and manipulative. Was he implying that her and Judilay's bond was based on mere mimicry?

Why would Judilay do that? Was he simply experimenting, practicing his interpersonal skills? Her intuition rejected that notion. Maybe her latent ability contributed to their mutual attraction. Was it purely attraction? Infatuation? No. It was a deep connection like recognizing a kindred spirit. Entanglement.

She thought of the belief in reincarnation, the spirit traveling through time in successive bodies in a quest for enlightenment. Touching on that was the suggestion of soulmates seeking out one another across various incarnations. Was something like that at work here? How? Weren't Synons outside the plane of planetary life within this universe? How could a human and Synon have encountered one another in past lives? It was possible if it had been between a human and an Earth-Synon. She wasn't entirely convinced of the reincarnation theory, even though it seemed to correlate with the universe's constant death and rebirth so apparent in Earth's natural cycles.

Lana's awareness shifted to a presence that seemed to be lurking in her mind.

"Lana? Want to share with us?" Mac's voice invaded.

Lana turned on him, eyes sparking. "Are you spying on my mind?"

"Of course not! How could you even suggest such a thing?"

"Something is!"

Tami looked concerned. "We must ask permission unless we're confronted with an urgent danger. May I scan your mind? You can will it to partition off all but the area where you sense the presence."

Lana was reluctant. "Maybe it's Judilay. This all concerns him too."

"He would ask permission."

Lana knew she was right. If not Judilay, who? A shudder wracked her body.

Tami moved toward Lana. "Does the presence feel friendly or menacing?"

Lana pushed herself to lightly touch it, then exclaimed, "Warmth! Love! No sense of menace. It must be Judilay!" She addressed it, "Judilay? Is that you? You know my mind is never closed to you." There was no sign of response, but Lana instantly knew what she must do. She turned to Tami. "It's not Judilay." She beamed. "I think I know who it is, and Earth told me her wishes."

CHAPTER EIGHTEEN

Roger Singleton was having second thoughts. A flurry of ideas had propelled him to hastily draw up plans—until reason crept in. His preliminary designs could revolutionize humanoid robots, but they provided no structure for cyborgs, which was what he needed for transplanting his own brain and having it function indefinitely. The necessary processes would require many expert workers, but Singleton was certain that confidentiality would be ensured by his methods that compartmentalized all elements, so that no person knew how the component on which they worked fit into the finished product or the purpose of that product.

A disturbing reality dawned on Singleton. He must rely solely on Dr. Gabe Jackson to implement the entire process of moving his living brain into the cyborg machinery, conducting the myriad intricate connections, and guaranteeing that the completed cyborg controlled by Singleton's brain functioned properly. Jackson had admitted to being an extraterrestrial. Even though Dr. Jackson had built a sterling career developing limb prosthetics attached to brains in ways that allowed functionality, he had not completed an entire brain-to-body connection. No one had. At least no human. Could he trust that Jackson would actually fulfill his part of the bargain? Logistically, how would it be accomplished? When? It would mean the death of Singleton's body. Could Jackson keep the brain alive long enough to complete the extensive process? Would he call upon others of his kind, or their technology, to help? Would they see the value in keeping Singleton's mind active if the rest of humanity perished? What would be his value to them?

Singleton worked himself into a state of anxiety. Did he really want to be the only human mind left? What would it be like on Earth with none of its natural biological life? Freezing and/or boiling? Why would any entity want to be there? Aliens might covet raw materials, especially minerals, that would be available for their harvesting, until extreme climate and planetary conditions began to degrade or alter all natural resources. Of course, to streamline their operations without interference the extraterrestrials would want to eliminate Earth's most industrious species.

Panic consumed Singleton. Should he alert the authorities? What could they do against the full range of whatever advanced technology the aliens surely possessed? Why risk alerting the authorities when they might uncover information that could lead to the discovery that he had kidnapped Emma Goodsen? He could be imprisoned for a considerable time before Earth deteriorated beyond repair. Time that he could be enjoying life as it was.

Despite the dire prospects his imagination had conjured, Singleton's survival instinct continued to drive him to find or create any opportunity to ingratiate himself with the aliens. Would they want robots he could provide them that would make it easier for them to fulfill their mission on Earth? They had shown him a small ship purported to be conscious. His contact with them had been with what they called projections. Were they pure consciousness without bodies? If so, he could devise robotic bodies to suit their needs. Could they already do that?

The major quandy was whether he was ready to betray his own species. If they were doomed, there was no choice. Then again, was it possible to counter the aliens in some way if people united? Anyone able to facilitate such an outcome would be in a position of significant power.

■　　■　　■

"No way!" Jeff shouted, rising from his chair and punching the air with his fist. Mac, Tami, and Lew flinched at his vehement response. He sat back down in his chair on the front porch of the Synon farmhouse. "After we all uprooted our lives and spent a year dealing with Bandela's destruction, you expect the Tech Team to allow him to live among us? I mean, we love it here and wouldn't go back, but his presence could not be tolerated."

"We understand," Tami admitted. "It had to be considered. We know energy can't be expended to confine him in the Realm again, and we can't let those who helped us after his initial capture know he escaped from the Realm. Does anyone have any other suggestions?"

Lew spoke up. "Bandela insists he wants to help. And he was able to connect with Earth. She wouldn't have spent her energy showing him the near future if she didn't see some way he can help. And I think that only The Living World could have accomplished both Tami and Bandela's journeys."

Mac snapped. "Nevertheless, he must be controlled, but our capacity is stretched thin already."

Lew agreed. "That's a strong point. Could we put him on an isolated island?"

Tami shook her head. "We'd still have to expend resources to guard him. And how could he be of use that way?"

Mac had been deep in thought. "People helped us contain him before. I can assemble a small, competent, and trustworthy team for that. Although he was previously in a Faraday cage that prevented him from using his Synon power. Even on an isolated island he'd require containment. He could just be a prisoner with no benefit to us."

"Like teaching Uniques," Lew added.

"We can't trust him anywhere near Uniques," Jeff growled.

Tami said, "He also insisted that Bret and his followers would help if he led them." She replied to her own comment before the others could. "No. That's too dangerous. Their long history here would enable them to communicate effectively with Uniques, but if just one strayed from the mission, it could prove catastrophic."

Lew spoke up, "What if we just enlisted Bret? He and Josh Jackson could train a lot of Uniques quickly."

Jeff's eyebrows rose. "All on that remote island with mortals as guards?"

"Could we spare two strong Synons? They and the mere mortals I have in mind can control two strong Synons."

"If the Synon guards can also train Uniques," Tami mused.

Jeff persisted. "What if Bandela and Bret corrupt the Uniques?"

Mac answered, "That's why strong Synons must embed links in their minds, with at least one fully focused on them at all times. When they're not working with Uniques, they'll be in a Faraday cage. Does anyone have an alternate plan?"

"I think taking Uniques to a remote island with Bandela and Bret is impractical," Jeff said. "What island? Where? Who administers it? Can we build what we need and keep it supplied?

Wouldn't those supply runs provide escape opportunities to Josh and Bret? It seems like a logistical nightmare."

Mac gave him a sly smile. "Don't you know by now how far my trusted contacts reach? There are suitable places that will satisfy all of your questions."

*   *   *

After lengthy discussions with Bandela-Josh Jackson laced with "carrots and sticks," Josh was persuaded to comply with their plan. He continued to insist that both he and Bret were serious about doing whatever they could to alleviate the crisis faced by Earth and all those who depended on her, including the two of them. To demonstrate their compliance, the two agreed to imprisonment while the island was being readied.

Everyone at the camp was surprised when Annilu volunteered to be one of the Synon guard-instructors. "I can contribute much more in that role than I do here," she said when asked why she wanted the assignment.

This presented something of a dilemma for the camp's Synon leaders who had continued to be disappointed by Annilu's lack of rapport with people. She would be very effective as a guard, but they questioned her ability to effectively bond with and train Uniques. How could they gracefully reject her request? Should they give her a chance?

*   *   *

Another unexpected situation came up when Mac approached the person he wanted to supervise Josh and Bret's island prison: Cal Booker. Mac realized that would remove one of his most valuable people from the camp. Suki seemed genuinely invested in their cause, and at the camp she was well protected from Singleton. Cal would be best utilized overseeing the island.

Mac went to Cal's apartment to brief him on his new mission. Cal hesitated to confirm his acceptance of the post. "Suki needs my support; she feels out of place and wonders why she was brought here."

Mac bristled. "We need her communication skills, especially now as we put out our cover story."

Cal nodded. "Have you explained that to her?"

Mac wanted to move on. "I thought we had. Cal, this is of utmost importance. You are by far the most qualified and trustworthy person to oversee this operation. We need you to jump in right now."

At that moment, Suki walked in. "Hi, Sweetie. Ready for…?" She stopped mid-sentence. "Oh. I'm sorry. I didn't know you had a meeting this morning." She looked flustered. Both men stood.

Mac's bushy eyebrows had leapt almost to his hairline when he heard the term of endearment she directed at Cal. He quickly recovered, taking charge. "Cal is taking on a vital mission for us."

"Oh," Suki looked worried.

Cal's long legs took him to her in a couple of strides. He placed his arms on her shoulders. "Bandela, as Josh Jackson, and his sidekick Bret are being imprisoned on a remote island where they'll train Uniques."

"Well, what could go wrong there?" Suki quipped.

Mac intervened. "Cal possesses the best range of qualifications to oversee it. He'll be accompanied by another human guard and two Earth-Synons, along with a small support staff."

Stricken, Suki had broken away from Cal to sink onto the sofa. "How long will this be for?"

"No time limit," Mac asserted. "It depends on the level of cooperation we get from the renegades."

Suki looked like she was about to cry. Cal sat next to her, taking her hand. "It's not set in stone."

Mac struggled to control his reaction. He would never get used to the way people put personal feelings above duty. First Judilay and Lana and now this. He was astonished that Cal and Suki had become a couple. Now neither would be effective if separated. He put on a sympathetic expression. "I'm sorry. I had no idea how close you had become. We're at a crucial juncture. Many are being asked to put personal concerns aside for the good of all. Suki, we need your communications skills more than ever as we roll out our cover story."

Suki wasn't ready to accept that. "Won't you need internet and phone service on that island? After we implement the cover story, couldn't I work there as well as here? I could even document the process of training Uniques and their personal progress."

"We need you stateside to get the cover story out, and you must understand how dangerous Josh and Bret are. We couldn't allow your presence on that island."

Concern apparent on his face, Cal spoke, "Suki, Mac is right. You've had limited contact here with Synons, all of them benevolent. These two we'll be guarding are abominations. The Unique training will begin as a very small-scale experiment with at least one of our Synons always present. It won't be a place for you. As much as we'll miss each other, you need to stay here."

Still sniffling, Suki stood. "Okay. Will we at least be able to video chat?"

■ ■ ■

Mac was anxious to begin disseminating the cover story. It was imperative to put a halt to all the public conjecture and conspiracy stories beginning to spread. If they could take the public attention off it for a while, something else would pop up to take precedent. Humans had short attention spans.

The answer appeared when Judilay asked for a video conference with him, Tami, Lew, Jeff, Emma, and Lana. Brimming with curiosity, the group met in the secure screening room.

When Judilay appeared, Mac bellowed, "Okay. What's so important?"

Judilay grinned broadly and began calmly explaining the processes that had been devised and were in use within the global network now called "Operation Unique" to debrief the image recipients coming forth: tell them the truth. There was no need to disclose the existence of Synons. They were not involved in what happened. An exceptional human Unique had been so moved by an image of the lovely, but vulnerable, Earth from space that he inadvertently transmitted it. No reason to say it appeared to have been a kind of out-of-body experience. He just saw the picture.

The story was constructed to convey that a few people aware of their telepathic abilities were in communication and had been able to mentally connect with the sender. Then realizing that many telepaths who were unaware of their ability could have seen it, they established the website which the sender agreed to mentally broadcast, knowing that only others like them would receive it. As responses came in, they built a coalition to unite and help them.

Emma was ecstatic. She jumped up, pumping her fist in the air.

Jeff was skeptical. "That seems plausible so far. Much better than a hoax. But what about when you tell them they are needed to unite and telepath with Earth? Will that seem too far-fetched for them? Won't some of them blab about it? Post it everywhere?"

Tami concurred. "Jeff is right. I was thinking the same thing."

"So were we," Judilay's expression was almost smug. "We don't touch on it. We're constantly refining our selection process to separate out those who seem stable and open-minded, especially those most concerned with what's happening to our planet. This can make your jobs easier. All of them will get training on how to manage their telepathy, including psychological support. We choose only the most likely candidates to move on to the Earth Project. Those will eventually have to be told at least about Earth's consciousness, and maybe Synons, so the screening process is crucial."

Mac was nodding, a light smile curving his lips. "This could solve our cover story problem. We can get it out rapidly. The world already knows there are telepaths among them. We'll just confirm it. End of public conjecture."

Emma was practically bouncing. "We need to talk to them. Get their plans."

Judilay responded. "We're working on a package we can share with you and other sites worldwide. I'm thrilled that you are in agreement. I have to admit that I was extremely upset at the suggestion of telling the public it was a hoax. I need to go now. I love and miss you all."

As the screen went black, silence fell in the room for a moment until Emma exclaimed, "We can still be the center of Unique training in the U.S." She grinned. "Of course, everyone here will have to be extra careful to keep our Synon friends a secret."

Tami was pensive. "We'll need to move on anyway and turn this camp over to people. I must get back to the Realm as soon as I can."

"Oh no!" Emma ran to Tami and threw her arms around her.

Lew spoke. "Emma, we know you two have a special bond. Lew and I will still be around, but our attention is needed in many places." He paused, gazing at Jeff. "And Jeff as well."

"No! Can't he stay here and be our leader?" Emma pleaded.

"Jeff's path might take him in other directions," Mac mused. "At least for a time. Lana can remain here, but her focus must be continuous monitoring of Uniques and revising our training and counseling plans. We'll find a suitable Unique to lead you and to help other adults brought here to accept your authority as teachers. Right now I must discuss this with our Media Director."

"Huh? Who's that?" Jeff asked.

"Suki Kurosawa."

CHAPTER NINETEEN

Jeff was disturbed by the references to his future. He just wanted to stay there in his cabin with Marie and Cosmos. Why couldn't he lead the camp Uniques? Emma had noted that they could become the center of training in America. How would Marie react if he were again sent somewhere on a mission that he might not even be able to discuss with her? He was encouraged that she had been enlisted to oversee the communications among the camp and far-flung sites that were now united as Operation Unique. That was an important job for which she was well qualified.

His transmission of the Earth image seemed to erect a new barrier between them. Marie had been supportive afterward. She was the only one who heard him berating himself for being so impulsive and lacking in judgment. Nevertheless, Jeff knew that Marie was sad that so many had been able to perceive his image while she couldn't. He sensed her increasing feeling of being excluded. Jeff resolved to argue to become the lead camp trainer.

■　■　■

"Is no one here doing that now?" Suki did not react the way Mac had anticipated when told he wanted her as their Media Director. He expected excitement and gratitude.

"We've deliberately remained hidden. I've long been friends with Vera Schechner, and I ask for her help occasionally, more often to keep something out of the press."

Suki mused. "So now you have to get a story out to the public and need someone to implement it."

"Not just now. Once we go public we'll need to constantly monitor and guide press coverage of the ongoing Operation Unique project. Paramount will be reassuring ordinary people that Uniques pose no threat to them."

"How can we say that? We can't control them. They're human. Some will use it for their own purposes. That's what humans do."

"Are you saying you're reluctant to be our spokesperson?"

"I'll help with this initial announcement, but I can't be part of any guarantees."

Mac was irritated but saw her point. "I recognize that we can never monitor every Unique's actions. We just need time to get the most qualified for implementing the Earth Project. We don't know how long she can hold on."

Suki was stricken. "She. I still find that unbelievable." She hastily added, "But I accept it. What you're implying is that no other considerations can take precedent over that one mission."

"Yes. We all must focus. We can't create panic by telling people their world is about to become unlivable, but we can stress what scientists show us about human action's detrimental effects and how rapidly conditions are deteriorating. We are all experiencing it in real time with the consequences of a warming planet."

"We can't link that message with information about Uniques."

"No. We must avoid that. The climate message will be a different campaign."

Suki was chewing her lower lip. "I will commit to handling the telepath story. Will we call them Uniques publicly? That could immediately set off alarms. Think about all the mutants in comics and films. They tend to be the objects of fear and prejudice."

"That's always been an excellent entertainment metaphor for human prejudice in general, but you're right, now it's real. We've been using the term Unique to differentiate, just for simplicity. But that won't work publicly. I need to run this by Tami and Jeff. And maybe the human team members to get a better handle on potential reactions. Would you like to be in that meeting?"

"Sure."

■　　■　　■

"Must be something really important," Marie noted as she and Jeff walked into the gathering hall. "Looks like Mac invited everybody."

Growing weary of meetings, Jeff's hand idly raked through his hair. "He said it was our final step in preparing Suki's presentation to the media. Maybe he just wants everyone to know what's going out before they see it along with the rest of the world."

They arrived in the gathering hall, greeted the others already there, and took seats.

"Mac opened the meeting with a recap of what had been decided about the media story. They were all relieved that the hoax idea had been dropped, especially since so much was already circulating about global telepathic exchanges.

Suki asked, "Will we publicly identify Jeff as the telepath who transmitted the image?"

"No. No." Mac asserted. "We'll keep that confidential, at least for now. But he is the perfect person to be the public face of our organization. And Suki will be the professional who directs our public efforts."

The group knew about Suki's involvement in the prior year's events, but had wondered why she was brought to the camp aside from Mac's story that she was in danger.

Emma piped up, "Will you tell them about Synons?"

"Oh no!" Mac bellowed. "Everyone must take extra care to never let anything slip about us. That's imperative. None of us relish misleading people. Unfortunately, it's what we have always had to do here in order to fulfill our mission.

"Learning that some of them are telepathic is enough for the human race right now. They couldn't deal with knowledge of Synons. It would totally destroy our mission for them to realize that people they knew, liked, trusted, were not actually human."

Hoping to move things along, Jeff spoke up, "So the primary question is how we will publicly define the Uniques. We should just say telepaths instead of Uniques. That's more than weird enough for most people. We can't conjure up any ideas about us being mutants." He winced. "Besides, we have no idea of how many people actually do have latent telepathic abilities."

Obviously struggled to control her expression, Marie murmured, "I don't think we should ever touch on that. It's cruel to lead people on when we have no evidence." Feeling like his heart was breaking, Jeff took her hand.

Lana had been scrolling. Now she interjected, "I'm looking for another word for telepath. People lump together all kinds of things into what is commonly called ESP—extrasensory perception. For lack of a better word, I think it's a good idea to simply use the term telepath, which means thought transfer. That's what we need to stress. They can't affect matter with their minds. No hurling boulders or starting fires. Just talking to each other mentally."

Suki was furiously typing on her laptop. "That's great. I'll use it. Thank you."

Tami stood. "So we're in agreement?" She looked at everyone. There were nods and affirmative murmurs around the table. "Any other comments on this topic?"

Mac stood as Tami sat, relinquishing the floor. "I want to thank you all for your input on this vital matter. Suki can finalize her message and send it out. It will be under the revised name of our global organization."

Surprised, Suki asked, "What is it?"

Mac shrugged. "So far every idea we suggest is already some kind of organization, with many uses trademarked. We need to think out of the box."

Suki threw up her hands. "So how can I put it out?"

"Work on your copy. By the time it's ready we'll give you a name."

Marie popped up, "What about 'We All Speak?' I just did a quick search and nothing with that name came up." Smiles broke out.

"I like that," Lana said. "It connotes unity."

Annilu had been silent. Now she spoke up. "But this whole issue came about by the transmission of an image, not words."

Jeff had been sitting with eyes closed, they popped open and his voice rang out. "Confluence." Varied comments overlapped as the group reacted, many suggesting words to accompany his suggestion. Tami, Mac and Lew locked eyes. Jeff rose and said quietly. "That's it. Just that word. Confluence."

Tami and Lew joined Jeff and Mac as the only ones at the table standing. Tami addressed everyone, "We believe Jeff speaks not only for himself." A few gasps were heard. Jeff didn't react.

Several people furiously searched on their devices.

Suki spoke in a business-like manner, "Lots of uses of the word Confluence, including organizations, but I don't find just the word alone. Haven't checked trademarks yet, but can you even trademark one word? Looks like we're good to go." Her chair slid back as she closed her laptop in preparation to leave.

Tami's serene voice halted her. "A few more minutes, please. I think Jeff has more to say."

Jeff looked lovingly at Marie and then affectionately at the group. He cleared his throat. "Uh, I think I'm supposed to lead this Confluence." He shrugged. Marie's sharp intake of breath was audible. Awestruck gazes turned on Jeff. He stood, dazed.

"Of course!" Emma exclaimed.

As the group drifted out, Jeff sat next to Marie, taking her hands in his. "Marie, it was like I was channeling some other entity, but not in a scary way. It was reassuring. Maybe it was just instinct, but I think it was Earth. From now on, I must do what seems right to me. One thing for sure, no matter where I go, or what I do, you and Cosmos will be with me."

Marie's laugh tinkled. "Maybe that's why he took to the leash so easily when most cats his age, especially ferals like he was, would have no part of it."

The three Synon leaders had also stayed. They gathered behind Jeff and Marie and hugged them both. "Come with us," Tami whispered. "You too, Marie."

■   ■   ■

As Jeff, holding Marie's hand, followed the three Synons through the woods surrounding the camp, he tried to shield the tumultuous thoughts he couldn't control. He knew his friends didn't eavesdrops on other's minds—unless there was a compelling purpose behind it. Did his mental state meet that threshold?

From time to time, Marie glanced at him worriedly. His expression and body language lay bare his mood to her. Conflicting emotions tormented Jeff. Forefront was a palpable urge to run far away, alternating with exuberance at the path ahead of him that could change the world. But why him? What had made him speak up like that? He had inadvertently transmitted the image that was now bringing global Uniques together, but he was no leader. Sure, he had led in the Air Force and jobs. He wanted to lead the camp Uniques, but mainly to just stay among familiar people and places. Those were nothing compared to what he had just volunteered for. Jeff Hawke lead a global effort? Oh yeah, it's goal was only to prevent the world from becoming uninhabitable.

Marie wasn't reading his mind, but she knew exactly what he was thinking. She spoke softly, "Jeff, some force beyond us was speaking through you, just like you were led to send that image. I know that sounds like bad movie dialogue, but everyone knows it, especially the Synons and Uniques. Again, it sounds corny and overused, but I can't think of another way to say it; you've been chosen. And whatever or whoever chose you must know you're capable of achieving the desired effect. Who better to lead the Uniques that Earth has told us are the only ones who can help her? You're the first Unique." She caught herself. "I mean telepath."

Jeff dropped back a bit to put more distance between them and those ahead, although he was well aware that they had developed better hearing than people had. "I think Emma was before me. And we're just the first to come to the attention of these Synons. There must have been many more before us, probably throughout history."

"Doesn't matter. Remember that they tested you and Cosmos before you were in contact with Emma. And don't forget Tami targeted you before everything happened."

"Yeah. She was hunting people like me." He paused. "Marie, could these newest Uniques, uh, telepaths feel that? They might not all believe our story. They could start thinking that the image was a ploy to lure them out so we could use them."

"Some might. Those finally selected for the Earth Project should see it as an honor."

At that moment, the trees fell away to reveal a wide-open area so covered in wildflowers that they had no choice but to tread on some to weave their way through them. The Synon trio stopped at a wide creek emanating from two streams on the other side of a low waterfall.

As Jeff gazed at the sight, realization washed over him. He felt tears pricking behind his eyes. Everyone stood back to give him space. "A confluence," he whispered.

■　　■　　■

Before Suki was able to prepare and disseminate their public message, rumors took hold across social media and news outlets that trafficked in conspiracy theories, sparking fear that led to irrational actions across the world. Among the most vocal were those in the United States.

A large crowd assembled in front of the White House carrying placards and shouting for their government to protect them against the alien invasion. The extraterrestrials had boldly begun revealing themselves, taunting the world with their telepathic power, obviously the first of their superhuman capabilities to be demonstrated. Some of the crowd rushed the barriers that had been set up in front of the tall fence surrounding the White House grounds. Outfitted in protective gear, Secret Service tactical details formed a tight line between the barriers and the fence. Tension electrified the atmosphere.

       ▪   ▪   ▪

Roger Singleton gleefully watched the activity in Washington unfold on his huge television. His covert work to inform the public of the alien presence on Earth was showing results. He was still reluctant to drop his final card by revealing that he was acquainted with at least one of the invaders. That should wait for the appropriate moment when it could reap the most results.

Singleton continued to ponder the purpose of Dr. Gabe Jackson disclosing to him that he was an alien. Was he seeking an ally? Was it an attempt at intimidation? He hadn't heard from Jackson since his visit to the mountain facility and one subsequent call asking Singleton to modify his cyborg plans. Singleton had been irritated at the suggestions. They veered from his objective. He now realized that Jackson was thinking about robots for himself and the aliens, not Singleton the human. If their actual nature was merely consciousness with no bodies, they would want protective, mobile housing for themselves. They might not have physical brains and nervous systems to delicately connect to what he was designing as a cyborg for himself.

A rare thought hit Singleton. Was he wading into new territory so uncharted that the risks couldn't be calculated? He was suddenly glad to have been careful to keep his manipulation of the anti-alien mob covert. Should he back off?

How could he extricate himself from building the bodies for an alien invasion and occupation or genocide? He had foolishly blabbed to Jackson about his encounter with the aliens and their sentient craft. Should he turn in Jackson? No. Leading authorities to Jackson could implicate him in the kidnapping of Emma Goodsen. Again he questioned his potential options. Did he want to be the only human left alive? And how long could he survive if the Earth became uninhabitable? His brain would still need oxygen which might no longer exist on the planet. He'd die anyway.

As yet, there was no evidence that extraterrestrials were behind the recent telepathic events, but what else could it be? He had seen and communicated with aliens. He still saw no way to convey that information to authorities without possibly incriminating himself. He would rethink his covert actions and keep as many options open as possible for his own survival.

CHAPTER TWENTY

"Breaking News" music and graphics interrupted YCN's regular broadcast. Even though he was not the anchor in that time slot, Jack Harvey's familiar face appeared, alerting viewers that something important was happening. Harvey had a long history with the cable news channel, but most recently had been moved out of primetime positioning in favor of younger, more diverse anchors. His sudden presence conveyed a sense of gravity, especially with long term viewers.

"YCN is presenting an exclusive interview of special global interest," Harvey's deep voice began. "I'm happy to introduce Suki Kurosawa." As she entered Harvey turned to her. "Suki, welcome."

Suki smiled and shook hands with Harvey. "Thank you."

"Suki, please share your message."

The shot cut from the two people to Suki alone. She looked into the camera directly at each viewer. "I have exclusive information from a new and important group working under the umbrella name of Confluence. In simple terms, that word means multiple things meeting to form one thing, like two small rivers joining to form one larger one. The members of this international group are average people who recently were thrust into the limelight by what now seems to have been a positive accident.

"You probably are aware of this story. Before providing vital details, I'll recap the events. An image of our own planet Earth from space, similar to this NASA photo, abruptly appeared in the minds of perhaps thousands of people worldwide." The image replaced her face. "I will now explain to you exactly how that happened, and the consequences."

The camera returned to Suki as she skillfully laid out the sequence of events. "One person's telepathic ability was confirmed when they were so moved by the significance of an image of Earth from space that they inadvertently transmitted it mentally to many others worldwide, demonstrating that they also were telepathic." She went on to describe how diverse people reacted to the receipt of the image.

"Now, some of them have united and are reaching out to provide comprehensive assistance to their new community with the goal of learning to control their ability and use it for the betterment of everyone."

The camera returned to Jack Harvey, now seated at a table. "What steps were taken?"

The camera pulled out to reveal Suki sitting across from Harvey. Suki related how the website was established and its address transmitted mentally, then implored those who had not received the telepathic messages not to clog the website. "As progress is made, efforts will be implemented to continue identifying and helping others who might have this ability."

The shot returned to Suki and Harvey seated across from one another. Harvey had another question. "Do we have any idea of how many of us might possess this capability?"

Suki smiled. "I suppose many of us are wishing we all had it, but as of now, science has no knowledge of how widespread this phenomenon might be, and what circumstances might trigger it. Research will continue, of course."

Harvey was nodding. "Understood. I'm sure this new situation, in which only some of us possess an ability, raises societal and ethical questions."

Suki responded, "Yes, definitely. The primary thing we must ensure is that this new ability should not be used in any way to do harm or for the personal gain of any individual. This fact must be amplified: these people can only exchange thoughts mentally. They can't affect matter or energy. They can't move or alter objects or living things, or cause events to happen. They can just communicate with their minds. Period."

"Excellent point that everyone should remember. Suki, I've known you throughout most of your career. How is it that you came to speak for this new group?"

She smiled warmly. "We have known each other a while. I'm proud of my affiliation with Your Cable News over the years. It's consistent devotion to the truth is what led me to release my information through this channel first. As for why I'm sitting here now with this story, it's simply through my being privileged to be a journalist. In this work, as you so well know, we come in contact with many different people. To me, this is one of the perks of my job. So, simply through a chain of interactions, I became acquainted with someone in this new group. I found their mission fascinating, and as I pursued more knowledge, my admiration for their goals took me a step beyond objective journalism to helping them with their communications."

"Thank you for being up front about your role with this organization. Do you have any further comments?"

"I do. As I stated when discussing the mission of Confluence, I'm concerned about the potential for their existence creating division in our society. Perhaps we should think of them having a special talent more than a special ability. We all have talents. My hope is that we can embrace and welcome these people as a potential benefit to our society and not fear or marginalize them."

"A wonderful note on which to end our interview. How can the public learn more about Confluence?"

Suki provided the address of a new, public, Confluence website, then concluded. "Jack, I'm grateful for this opportunity; we hope that YCN and other reliable outlets will share our information."

■　■　■

Despite the explanation from Confluence, frenzy was growing around Earth faster than their message was spread. The assumption that it would rapidly go viral on social media didn't materialize. Flashy posts containing wild theories and calls to action were more effective attention-grabbers.

The Washington demonstration was smoothly contained, while other world cities didn't fare as well. Destruction, looting, and violence erupted. Globally, signs and banners issued similar demands for protection from aliens, mutants, and other assorted allusions to "the other." However, in a few places, there were actually counter demonstrations asking for tolerance toward the telepaths.

The release of the official announcement both helped and hindered Confluence. It was apparent that large swaths of the global population didn't believe the cover story, as they continued to sensationalize alternate explanations. Among many of those who accepted the explanation, resentment and fear of the newly revealed mutants took hold.

Speculation that acquaintances and public figures were telepaths grew rampant. Suspicion damaged all kinds of relationships.

Within the Confluence coalition there was conflict and alarm. Disagreements flared over the new name and the dismissal of the term "Unique." Those who had come forth began requesting security. New contact dropped off, as those who were still unidentified stayed silent.

*　　*　　*

MacIntyre decided it was time to initiate his planned expansion of the Tech Center-Camp into the North American Confluence headquarters. Separately, he and Lewis Henderson had bought a large amount of land immediately surrounding that currently in use, careful to do nothing that could bring unwanted attention to their purchases.

As Mac laid out his plans, anticipation and excitement permeated the atmosphere. Everyone was more than ready to move forward, especially the three children who were now referred to as telepaths rather than Uniques.

Excited reactions were demonstrated by overlapping comments. Mac called upon his Synon vocal power, "Quiet! Everyone will have a chance to speak. Each one of you needs to apply your talent and experience toward making this plan a success. I know that logistics is the primary issue to tackle up front. We're in a remote place with one regional airport relatively close and, as of now, no passenger rail service. Roads are fine until visitors get near our location. Upgrading those final ones, especially on the land we own, will be priority.

"I'd like to diverge a moment here to stress where we are ready, primarily the significant upgrades to the communications and power grids made during our tenure so far.

"Now, back to access." He grinned. "Jeff and Mannie, as avid pilots, will be happy about this next phase. We will build our own airstrip." The two men he had mentioned whooped in glee. "It won't handle large planes but will accommodate adequate air traffic for people and supplies. Mannie, we know you've been missing urban life, especially your native New York. We hope you'll stick around here a while longer, since we'll need the expertise from your prior life as a pilot and air traffic control systems programmer." Mannie beamed. "I can find qualified, vetted personnel to man a small tower under your supervision. Of course, we'll purchase a couple more planes."

Son of a Jewish mother and a father whose parents were from India, Mannie had learned to adjust to diverse circumstances. He replied with a characteristic wry grin, "Well, I guess I can stand being in the boondocks for that assignment." He winked at Mac. "Maybe I should add a condition that I get to fly an aircraft when possible."

Mac laughed. "I'm sure that can be arranged."

The kids had been fidgeting, now they looked furtively at each other as they tried to conceal a mental conversation. Emma raised her hand. Mac raised his bushy eyebrows. "I know you're itching to speak, Emma. You have the floor."

Emma stood. Having passed her seventh birthday, she had grown, so that a good portion of her body was now visible above the top of the table. "How soon will we be getting students? Who will manage the training? It needs to be a Unique, not a Synon."

Mac sighed. "I admit that's a dilemma. Even though you're children, you three and Jeff are now the most experienced telepaths we have available. Jeff is needed for a wider role. Lana is an excellent candidate, but we need her to focus on the content of the training." Mac's use of the new term for their status was not lost on the kids. They were being told politely to change their own wording.

Lana spoke up, "I think I can do both. Hands-on experience working with trainees will provide the best feedback as to what's working and what needs to be changed. I also think the kids have practiced training each other to the point that they can command respect from adults who know nothing about controlling their ability. My hope is that we can find a few new adult telepaths who demonstrate a knack for leading and teaching others."

"Yes!" Emma pumped her arm in the air; Rick and Tina followed her lead. "Also to note," Emma interjected. "Rick might be only fifteen, but he's taller than many adults and has a really deep voice. Plus, he speaks Spanish and is a New Yorker who can stand up for himself."

"Okay." Mac took back control. "You all make valid points. Trying out your suggestions will give us time to develop more trainers. That's excellent. Our primary mission won't be interrupted while we deal with expansion tasks."

Tina raised her hand. Mac nodded toward the nine-year-old. She spoke in her soft Alabama accent. "This might not be a topic for today, but it's beginning to really bother us kids. When are you going to tell our families that this isn't really a summer camp and we won't be coming home soon?"

An irritated look flitted across Mac's countenance. "We know it has to be soon. Lana, can we call on your psychology knowledge to work out how to do that? It's imperative that they allow these children to continue their work." Lana nodded.

"Okay. We'll table that for now. Suki will continue the public relations campaign. We need Marie's expertise to enable a stronger continental communications network."

As Mac had rattled on, handing out assignments to all the people present, Chris Mills sat silently, looking at the table, absently twisting the blond ponytail that hung over one shoulder. He was visibly startled when Mac's voice rang out his name. "Chris, your knowledge and creativity were instrumental in rescuing Emma last year, when we convinced Singleton that the small craft you had designed was actually of alien origin. Please feel free to offer any ideas or suggestions as we move forward. You also proved to have a talent for planning and over-seeing implementation as we built out the camp. I'd like to see you continue that. I think you'll like the architect I'm bringing in. She specializes in integrating structures and Nature."

Chris perked up. "Sounds good. I'll enjoy that."

A dour-faced Annilu raised her hand. Mac reluctantly acknowledged her. "Sir, is it confirmed that I'll be joining the island expedition as a guard?"

Mac had hoped to avoid her at this meeting, focusing on the humans. He, Lew and Tami were still grappling with how to best utilize Annilu. She had proven inept at interaction and integra-tion into human society. They had hoped the Synons who would guard Josh and Bret could also double as trainers for telepaths, but that could prove too ambitious. He hedged. "We'll discuss that later. Personnel allocation for that mission isn't complete. In fact, the scope of the mission is still under discussion. At any rate, we'll not waste any opportunities to take advantage of your attributes." Scowling, Annilu nodded.

CHAPTER TWENTY-ONE

While the multiple strands of Confluence plans were beginning to be implemented, there had been a lag in identifying new telepaths suitable to become trainers or move on to the Earth Project, presenting a window of time to interact with the children's parents.

It was difficult to gather all three families in one place at the same time, since they lived in Florida, Alabama, and New York respectively. Lew Henderson, whose easy, empathetic manner made him the best negotiator on the team, undertook that first task by inviting them all to the camp as guests. He was surprised that all were grateful for the invitation and eager to come. It was finally settled that all of them could be at the camp on an upcoming Sunday.

Mannie was pleased to be given a few days off to visit New York. On his return trip he would pick up the parents of Rick Gomez and fly them back in a plane Mac would lease. Jeff would fly the plane Mac owned first to Florida for the Goodsens, then hop over to Alabama to pick up Tina Adams's parents.

Upon arriving and being shown around, the parents all liked the camp's atmosphere, but were surprised to learn that their children were the only ones there. Shock followed surprise when they were told the camp's actual purpose and why Emma, Tina, and Rick were its first attendees.

They could only be convinced by witnessing a demonstration of the children's power.

■　　■　　■

Those gathered at the Confluence stood back respectfully, although a couple of them wore skeptical expressions. Holding hands, Emma, Tina, and Rick knelt on the bank of the creek flowing from the spring. The songs of birds accompanied the babbling water's music. The children's faces couldn't be seen, and no sounds were heard from their voices. Yet, as one, they shuddered, then sank so low their faces nearly touched the water.

Grabbing her husband's arm, Mrs. Gomez issued an exclamation in Spanish. Others gasped more quietly, but all six of the children's parents displayed visible reactions. Jeff and Lana moved up behind them, each placing their arms on the shoulders of a couple. Unable to hear their telepathic conversation, Mannie moved swiftly to encircle the third couple when he saw their action. Lew Henderson stood respectfully in the rear. Only a few minutes passed, but to the onlookers it seemed like hours. Each of them inwardly struggled with what they were watching and what it meant for their family.

Finally, the children stirred. The parents took a few steps forward but were gently restrained by the hands on their shoulders. From the forest just beyond the other bank a bright red cardinal gracefully swooped forward, landing next to the creek. He cocked his head, gazing directly at the three children sitting motionless on the opposite bank. They remained silent, locking eyes with the bird, then all three nodded. The bird swooped away, and the children climbed to their feet, turning to face the people watching them. As one, they bounded to their parents. The three camp people had moved back to give them privacy as the families embraced. All but Mannie knew the contact had been successful.

Human voices were now louder than the small waterfall. Emma's voice rose above the din. "Hush! Everybody settle down, and we'll tell you all about it!" The parents went quiet, a bit shocked at this seven-year-old's strong voice and manner. Emma motioned for the others to join them. Although Rick was the oldest and tallest, Emma was undoubtedly this trio's leader. "I wish you could have heard it. Please believe everything we tell you. We could never lie or even fib; it would injure Earth; she's so fragile." Tears ran down Emma's cheeks. Rick and Tina moved next to her and took her hands. She continued. "We tried to soothe her. Tell her to feel the love and concern for her all over the world. We said we'd found many more like us, but it would take a little more time for them to be able to talk to her." She wiped her face with her hand. "Rick, can you—"

Rick assumed the narrative, "At first, all we could focus on was the erratic movement we felt. She's having a harder time maintaining her rotation." The stunned parents began firing questions. Rick raised his hand. "It's nothing dangerous now. We monitor her and talk to her all the time. We'll make sure she doesn't get worse. But right now, we are all that she has for reassurance." He turned to Tina, silently asking her to take over.

Tina nodded and began speaking, "The good thing is that we felt a positive response from her. She knows there are many more like us. She insists that we're the only ones who can really help her. That's why it's so important for us to stay here and concentrate on her. And, of course, we hope to have some students soon. Lana will oversee that." She smiled up at the only other Black person that had remained at the camp after Judilay left. She knew he wasn't really a person, but she admired him because he had chosen to appear as one of African descent when on Earth. She had admired Lana from the first time she'd met the beautiful woman with her low-country accent. Tina addressed the parents, looking from one to another. "So, you see, you really need to support what we are and what we can do. We have the most important mission on Earth!"

Mr. Adams spoke in his soft Alabama drawl, "We will, honey! We're so proud of you. We just wish we had known how unusually special you are."

Mrs. Adams was crying. "I feel so terrible that you didn't feel like you could confide in us."

"I knew you wouldn't know what to do," Tina murmured. She paused a moment before adding, "I didn't want to worry you." She had almost blurted out that she had been discovered by an Earth-Synon reaching out for receptive minds, leading to her being invited to the camp. It had been decided that their parents could not know about Synons.

The parents began talking at once to their children. Mrs. Gomez reverting to her native Spanish, as she sobbed and hugged Rick. Her husband hung back a bit; a high school science teacher, he was skeptical by nature, especially about anything that couldn't be proven.

The Goodsens had always known their daughter was precocious, so weren't surprised when MacIntyre had first visited them about the camp for advanced children. Now, learning that she was additionally gifted with telepathy was somehow not shocking. However, theirs was a close-knit family, and Emma's continued absence would have an impact.

With an impish grin, Emma made a request of her parents. "Can you bring Fuzzy here to stay with me? I've practiced contacting him mentally, but I don't think he knows who I am. Jeff has mental conversations with his cat. I want to learn to communicate with all animals. Oh, and can Liam visit me?"

Gary, her father, laughed. "Just like a sister, asking to see her cat before she mentions her brother! Yes. We'll do both before school starts."

Tears brimmed in Nina Goodsen's eyes. "I know Liam misses you; of course, so does Fuzzy. It's harder to believe that people can mentally communicate with animals. Their brains function so differently. I'm amazed that Jeff converses with his cat. This is truly remarkable." She hugged Emma. "I feel so blessed to have you as a child. We'll do everything we can to support you."

Tears glistened in Emma's eyes. "I'm the one who's blessed to have you as my family. I miss you all so much. But I love the people here also, almost like family, including the—" she caught herself from saying "Synons." "—cranky old man, Mr. MacIntyre."

■ ■ ■

As the Confluence message gradually became widely circulated more people accepted it, especially those telepaths who had been reluctant to reveal themselves. A steady stream of them came forth.

Just as things appeared to be normalizing, a new alarm was spread by a young Earth scientist who disagreed with the policy of not disclosing the erratic planetary rotation. He posted to his personal social media accounts that a potentially dangerous situation was being kept secret. He thought he was being fair by including in his writings the scientific rationale for not sharing that Earth's rotation on its axis was slowing down and speeding up in an erratic manner that was abnormal, although said to be within acceptable parameters, and only registering on the most sensitive detectors. He conceded that it was imperceptible on the Earth's surface.

Had he stopped there, the post might have garnered sparce attention, but he thought it necessary to inform people of the potentially devastating consequence that would occur if the planet's rotation deviated to the point that it halted, even for one second. The young scientist described how everything would be thrown forward at a velocity as high as one thousand miles per hour. The Earth's surface, and everything on it, would be shredded and thrust into space, followed by the Earth's gravity seizing chunks of matter that had flown upward, causing it to rain back down, in time turning the surface into hot, liquified rock. His poor judgment further added to his error when he ended by making a joke that, of course, no one would be left to witness the later event, since everyone would have been pulverized in the initial moment when the planet's rotation momentarily ceased.

Even though few people first saw the post, some shared it to another select few. The mechanism by which one post winds up going viral moved slowly for a short time, until more and more people shared it. Eventually, media and individuals with sizeable followings found it, and so it followed the path of so many of its predecessors.

This new revelation caused more panic than the news of telepaths among them. People paid no attention to the scientific explanation that the anomaly fell within normal parameters, posing no threat. The graphic description of the demise of life on Earth that could result from the situation was mangled in retelling. Tabloid headlines, irresponsible talk-radio and podcast hosts, and television commentators screamed that the end was near.

The young scientist who had caused the uproar was rapidly dismissed, ending his career just as it was getting started. He tried to pass himself off as a whistleblower to little result. The story was simply too far-fetched for reputable media who, instead, competed for the leading authorities on the subject as guest commentators.

Most governments hastily attempted to ease the panic with accurate information. Some elected officials demanded investigations of the scientists their governments funded. Why had they not warned those responsible for public safety? A few within parties in opposition to those in power disregarded the truth and grabbed the opportunity to sling accusations of government incompetence. Others used it to question the efficacy of science itself, linking it to what they saw as questionable assertions surrounding the topics of climate, the environment, and other natural phenomena.

At the fringes, conspiracy theories sprang up attributing the story as yet another sign of extraterrestrial activity, this time much more ominous.

■ ■ ■

Roger Singleton latched onto the extraterrestrial angle, even though he was unsure if it could be true. His rationale for disregarding his prior misgivings was that any publicity that accentuated the alien danger could deter them. Even though humans might not possess the means of physically defeating the extraterrestrials, increased vigilance and attention could make it more difficult for them to continue whatever their mission was on Earth.

He needed to be careful using his influence in support of the alien theory. It was crucial to avoid tipping off Gabe Jackson of his involvement, potentially leading to extraterrestrial retribution. Singleton would attempt no further communication with the roboticist. Hopefully, Jackson would be too busy to check up on the progress of the robotic body he assumed Singleton was designing.

Although the Japanese operative Akari had been ineffective in her mission to find information about Suki Kurosawa, she had an excellent record at discretely disseminating propaganda in the most effective places. He called her.

A day passed before Akari replied to his voice message. She was curt and distant.

"Akari," he crooned, "I was rude and unprofessional about your failure in Japan. I realize that my request was not necessarily one that could easily be accomplished. Now I hope you're available for an assignment that calls upon your strongest assets." Akari remained silent. Singleton went on to explain what he wanted her to do.

She was quiet a while before responding. "That will be a simple task, Mr. Singleton. Please send me any specifics. Shortly after, you'll begin to see and hear results. Do you still have the data for depositing my fee?"

"Of course. You'll receive a partial payment right away, followed by the remainder when I'm satisfied. I'll send you my further instructions now and will look forward to soon seeing the consequences of your efforts."

■　　■　　■

As a longtime renegade, Akari had rejected the purpose of the Realm and its inhabitants yet was unable to shed her innate

Synon traits. Fully aware that the Earth was certainly in a condition that posed a danger to her own continued existence, Akari set out to fulfill Singleton's mission in a manner that would satisfy him while subtly exposing its fallacy.

Meanwhile, she would alert Bandela and the Synons that she knew were behind the Confluence group. This was a matter grave enough to put aside differences and cooperate with the Realm in a common objective: survival.

CHAPTER TWENTY-TWO

Jeff felt like a pebble swept by river currents. Events moved too fast for him to adequately process. A jumble of feelings fought for his attention.

He was concerned about Marie and their relationship. They had discussed marriage but felt they didn't need outside affirmation of their bond. They agreed that they should make no major changes while their lives were so unpredictable.

Curious, Jeff had asked Lewis Henderson about traditional Cherokee marriage ceremonies, of which he could recall nothing from the many things he learned about his culture as he grew up. Although a Synon, Lew had lived as a Cherokee for centuries, through multiple personas. He had a deep understanding of traditional beliefs and practices.

The concept of a Cherokee couple's union differed from that of the modern American marriage; it incorporated their individual clans and required considerable preparation. Since Marie was not Cherokee and he was not involved with his clan, Jeff realized that they should not pursue it until he had time to rekindle ties with his people. His first cousin Sarah was his closest relative. His parents were dead. When his uncle, Sarah's father, passed, no close family was left in North Carolina. He would always be part of his clan and their tribal nation.

At present, Marie's skills were in demand working with Confluence's global communications. He knew she was at last feeling useful and enjoyed working with a network of diverse, interesting people. He resolved to make sure that she always had a productive and inclusive role in their activities.

Another matter weighed on Jeff. He was concerned about his cousin Sarah, whom he hadn't had a chance to speak with since Tami's strange disappearance. He had been assured that Lew's colleague had helped her cope by relating a concocted tale of Tami not actually vanishing. The story went that she had simply walked into the glare of the afternoon sun that obscured her figure as she entered the woods surrounding the pond behind the Dream Catcher.

As the account unfolded further, Tami had recently fallen and hit her head, an event of which Sarah was unaware. The effects were apparently more serious than had been thought, and while sitting outside the Dream Catcher, Tami's mind had temporarily blanked, and she just wandered off into the woods. The ringing of the phone in Tami's pocket brought her to herself. It was Lewis Henderson; he met her and took her to a hospital. Tami had totally forgotten about Sarah until Lew mentioned her. She was embarrassed; Lew suggested someone make apologies for her and let some time pass before rekindling her friendship with Sarah.

Jeff found the entire story a bit ridiculous, but Tami had approved it. Unfortunately, she had been caught up in subsequent events and was unable to reconnect with Sarah. As had he. Jeff recognized his own neglect of the person who was now his closest relative. He couldn't lose touch with her. He knew that Mac and

Lew were preoccupied with Confluence, but he felt like he had to let them know how he felt.

■　■　■

Jeff decided it was time to discuss Sarah with Mac and Lew and asked them to stay after a status meeting. Both knew from his demeanor that something was bothering him.

He was taken aback at Mac's reaction when he asked for advice on how to keep Sarah as part of his life and reassure her that he would always be there for her. "You must realize that you can't always honor that kind of promise. There will be times you can think of and do nothing except your mission. We're trying to save life on Earth. For humans, is there anything more important?"

Jeff bristled. "Of course not. And I am dedicated to that mission. Nevertheless, I will not abandon my cousin."

Mac snapped, "Jeff, do you think you're the only one who must put those you care for in the background for the sake of a crucial mission?"

Jeff sensed something left unsaid in Mac's outburst. Had he cared for someone he was unable to bring into his life? "Mac, I was in the military. We learned that duty was our first priority. But whatever we were called upon to do would ultimately be for the sake of those we loved. My loved ones are part of the world I'm dedicated to saving."

Mac started to speak, but Lew cut him off. "No, Mac. He's right. We can empathize only to an extent. We can't feel what a human does regarding family. Jeff's concern for Sarah will affect his ability to focus on the work at hand."

Jeff offered a potential solution. "I did tell Sarah I moved here for a classified government job, and that Marie was part of the team. She understood that I couldn't talk about it and might not always be available. I can tell her that it concerned my telepathy. Is that okay?"

Mac responded, "I see no problem in your explaining to Sarah that you recognized your ability before the infamous image and had made contact with a few others that you've been working with. Now they've asked you to be a leader for Confluence and you want to do it. However, you want to stay in touch with her."

■ ■ ■

When Jeff had assumed leadership of this emerging group it had not occurred to him that it would entail public speaking, which he detested. He balked at the idea.

Suki offered to give him a crash course that would enable him to feel comfortable in that role. Aware that he would have to speak for Confluence, Jeff reluctantly agreed to let her help him.

Suki put Jeff through his paces, throwing rapid-fire questions at him, interrupting his answers, contradicting him. She had a cowbell that she rang each time he said "uh, um," or repeated phrases and words like "you know" or "and." She stressed that a brief pause was best when searching for the right word. It could be used for effect. "Don't try to be formal," she ordered. "It's all right to use slang and talk the way you normally do. It shows who you are, a regular person, like those hearing your words."

He tried not to let her teaching style rattle him. She was the pro at this, after all. At times, he became exasperated but tried to ease out of it with humor. Suki was already setting up interviews. He had to be prepared.

■ ■ ■

People began insisting they could feel the Earth's erratic movement, despite daily media and governmental reminders that it was impossible.

However, those reliant on precisely accurate clocks did see changes. The length of each day could no longer be calculated in advance. Even fractions of seconds could affect sensitive mechanisms and processes that relied on precise synchronization.

Day and night were determined by the position and rotation of Earth on its axis in relation to the sun. It was this process that had become erratic when compared with trends in rotational rate tracked over time. A second factor, unrelated to the current issue that determined the day's length, was the Earth's orbit around the sun; it affected seasons and their accompanying shortening or lengthening of days.

Of course, many people didn't bother learning these basics.

In his strategy, Singleton utilized shared human traits that led people to believe unsubstantiated stories over narratives that relied on facts, usually requiring attention to understand. Following Singleton's instructions, Akari established a social media blitz under a bogus organization purported to be run by technicians, teachers, and scientists endeavoring to provide information to the public that was withheld by conventional institutions.

Akari was aware that Singleton and Bandela's persona, Dr. Gabe Jackson, had met and were working together on a project. However, Singleton was unaware that she knew this, and so did not tell Akari not to involve Dr. Jackson. He was the first person she contacted.

■　　■　　■

Now wearing the persona of Gabe Jackson's son, Josh, Bandela was in custody with no access to electronics, although not imprisoned within a Faraday cage that blocked all electrical transmission, including telepathy. He and Bret were held in a special section of a secure military base's brig, with human and Synon guards, arranged through trusted allies within MacIntyre's government affiliation.

The two personas were irritated and surly at the treatment. They were frustrated at the delay in moving them to the island where they were supposed to have more freedom and the opportunity to train newly discovered telepaths. They complained that the considerable capabilities they had offered were not being taken advantage of. They were provided with reading material, so when Jackson saw the reports on Earth's rotational problem he offered to craft scientifically acceptable wording that could explain the situation to lay people in efforts to tamp down panic. MacIntyre accepted it as a gesture of cooperation.

Housed in a separate cell from Bret, Josh was able to focus more on his embedded link to Singleton's mind; it provided endless amusement as Singleton's thoughts flitted between contradictory positions. Now Singleton's chaotic mind was becoming an irritation, and Josh tamped down the connection.

As Josh reclined on his cot, drafting his article, a distinct sensation alerted him that someone was attempting to mentally communicate with him. He had raised his barriers to keep the Synon guards out of his mind, even though he realized that they knew when he conducted mental conversations. Whoever was requesting entry now was obviously another strong Synon. Curious, he opened a sliver of a channel and was surprised to perceive Akari.

"What's going on?" she demanded. "Your phone is off with no voicemail available. Your email account has been closed."

He didn't bother to answer her. "Are you calling on behalf of Singleton?"

"I do have a new assignment from him that might interest you."

"Why would I care?"

"I assume you're familiar with the Earth's erratic rotation and know it's been leaked to the public."

Josh took a moment to compose his response before replying. He didn't want to let on to her than he had been reading Singleton's mind. "Yes to both parts of your query. Is Singleton meddling in the issue?"

"Of course. He hired me to disseminate his version aligned with rumors that extraterrestrials are behind that and the telepaths."

Josh snorted a laugh. "As Dr. Jackson, I told him I was an alien. We're supposedly working together on a robotics project."

Akari stated, "He never mentioned you."

"I'm no longer Dr. Jackson, anyway. I'm his son, Josh."

"To confirm. He thinks you're an alien entity from another planet. He knows nothing about Synons."

"To my knowledge that's correct. Why does he want to link aliens to this new phenomenon?" He was all too familiar with Singleton's irrational thought patterns, but was fishing for what she knew.

"I have no idea. I suppose he has no inkling of the actual nature of Earth, or how its teetering on the brink of losing control of life sustaining processes. That is of concern to me since it affects my existence."

Josh was relieved by her statement. Like him, she appeared to see that Synon existence was in jeopardy along with Earth's life forms. "He's such a fool. It might be another ploy to get the attention of aliens. He wants to ally with them to save his own skin when they do whatever he imagines they plan here."

"Could it be revenge? He's livid that the so-called aliens he met haven't been back in touch and accepted his offer to be their guide."

Josh replied, "He holds grudges and is vengeful. This could be bad. If too much noise is made about extraterrestrials, people will demand more investigation. No one can be allowed to inadvertently discover Synons. That would be bad for all of us."

"My plan is to blanket the fringe platforms and avoid mainstream media. I can show him copious posts and articles that should satisfy him. Authorities will pay no attention to the crazies who scream for them to root out the extraterrestrials." She paused. "Do you intend to break off contact with him as Dr. Jackson?"

"Yes. I must. I told him it could be difficult, if not impossible, to reach me. He seemed to understand my inferences."

"Do you have any contact with the Synons who masqueraded as extraterrestrials in order to rescue the child Singleton kidnapped, or those behind this new Confluence group?"

A bitter smile curled the lips Akari couldn't see. "Yes. I can reach all of them."

"They distrust me, but I need to convince them that I'm on their side in this matter of protecting the Earth for our own survival. At any rate, they should know what Singleton's doing."

"I assume you're working as the Japanese woman Akari. Give me your cell number. I'll convey it to them along with what you've told me today. As for me, for the time being our present mode of conversation will probably be the only way you can communicate with me." Once he had her phone number, he shut her out of his mind.

Josh lay back and smiled then pressed the button to talk to his guards.

CHAPTER
TWENTY-THREE

In the wake of the attack by Earth-Synons that freed Bandela, the Synons who collectively held the Realm together had difficulty maintaining cohesiveness. Power was diminishing in concert with Earth's duress. The Realm could not survive if any additional Synon energy left, so they formed tightly bound groups with Earth-Synons to help in multiple-pronged efforts.

TuMa'Aye Gra'Vay's absence contributed to their distress and was felt most keenly by Tork. He had tried not to hound her but now was concerned about the amount of time she had been away. He gave in to the urge to contact her. "I apologize for interrupting, but I must apprise you of the situation here."

The Tami Graves persona echoed in his mind. "I'm amazed that you were able to go this long without nagging me. I was preparing to come to the Realm, but as you know, things have become very complicated here, and I've been delayed."

"There's too little energy left in the Realm for complication," Tork retorted. "We could literally disappear in the near future."

"It's that dire?"

"We sense the void not only closing in, but pricking at us from within."

There was a long pause as Tork withdrew enough not to invade her contemplation before she spoke again. "We have Bandela. It's a long, somewhat surprising story, which I suppose is why I haven't taken the time to tell you. He professes to have repented, but since we can never trust him, I must ensure that controls on him are established. There is slow progress otherwise, but I think the Earth-Synons will soon be able to handle it, especially since we're enlisting human telepaths. I'm always aware that Earth and the Realm are barely holding on. Neither has any power to spare the other.

"Earth's issues have multiplied. Only a handful of human scientists recognize the wobble in her rotation, and certainly not to the extent that we do, but the situation was leaked to the public. People, of course, are acknowledging the frequency and breadth of disasters induced by climate change, although too many insist it's short-term weather events. They can't really attribute the rise in shifting tectonic plate and volcanic activity to weather, but those events often occur in sparsely inhabited places and don't get as much public attention."

Tork sensed a touch of despair in her. He had spent enough time as a human to have formed empathetic reactions similar to emotions. It could too easily be contagious; he could spare no energy for it.

TuMa'Aye mentally responded. "I'm sorry if I'm transmitting what people call negative vibes. Knowledge and wisdom are becoming my enemies in the current state of this world. There is some good news. One of the Tech Team has suddenly bloomed as a telepath."

Faces of the Tech Team members flowed through Tork's mind. "Which one?" TuMa'Aye related Lana's story to him. "That's very encouraging. She radiates caring and empathy, along with her wry humor. Lana will be a valuable asset. Perhaps more like her will appear."

"I'll try to disentangle myself here as soon as possible," Tami promised. "I sorely miss the Realm."

Earth-Synons were already taxed, but TuMa'Aye Gra'Vay, still at the camp, sent out an urgent request for those not presently involved in current activities to go to the Realm immediately, prepared to share as much of their power as they safely could.

■   ■   ■

Tami gathered the tech-camp group to give final orders and bid farewell.

"I suppose you can't estimate how long you need to stay there," Emma said, her lower lip protruding.

With a wistful smile, Tami shook her head. Emma nodded, the tears she had tried to control now spilling from her eyes. Sitting next to her, Rick reached over and put his hand on her arm.

"We'll be in constant communication," Tami said as she nodded toward Mac and Lew. "There are many variables that must coalesce to complete this most urgent mission."

"Excuse me," Mac strode out of the room, phone to ear.

Tami continued speaking, "I'll miss all of you. It will be especially hard to be away from my human friends whose talents don't include telepathy."

"I don't know if mine is strong enough to reach to the Realm, anyway," Lana admitted.

"You can reach the Bahamas," Emma reminded her.

"Yeah, but it's on this planet, in this universe," Lana quipped.

"Annilu, your strength is needed in the Realm rather than on the island team. You'll go there with me to use your strength to the best advantage. I'll notify Tork."

Annilu became defiant. "So you're issuing me an order?"

Mac's face clouded. "I'd suggest you learn to display a little respect to those far more experienced than you. TuMa'Aye Gra'Vay is the most qualified of us to make such decisions."

Lewis Henderson interjected. "Annilu, this is an honor and an opportunity for you. It acknowledges your superb strength. You need to learn how to best utilize it. The Realm will be grateful for your presence."

Mac added, "Each of us must follow the path for which we are most suited. Thank you for your efforts in the difficult mission you're now leaving."

Tami added, "This isn't banishment. You're needed there. It doesn't mean you won't return to Earth."

Annilu got up so abruptly that her chair slammed backward. She stalked out of the room.

When she was gone, Tami sat with her head in her hands. "People, how did we mess that up?"

Lana said, "She's immature. Like a spoiled child, she wants benefits without earning them."

Tami shook her head. "Her preparation was inadequate. This is a lesson for us. We need to revamp our processes for preparing Synons, who've been dormant a long time, to assume responsibilities. I'll convey that to Tork." Her expression softened. "Thank you. All of you people here. You continue to teach us."

Abruptly, the unfocused eyes of both Synons told the people that they were otherwise engaged.

They exchanged glances. Something was going on.

Jeff looked at Lana and shook his head as if warning her not to attempt to join the telepathic conversation that absorbed the Synons. Then, in an effort to divert attention, he spoke, "Suki's tortured me into something of an orator. The torment will continue with my upcoming interview at YCN." A wry smile twisted his lips.

Suki flashed an expression of mock exasperation. "He's prone to exaggeration." She rolled her eyes, then took on a serious look. "Jeff is a natural speaker. He'll do a fantastic job of expressing our message."

Tina's eyes widened. "Will they come here?"

"No," Suki replied. "Sorry to disappoint you, but we'll be going to their New York studio."

"Lucky you," Mannie murmured.

"It will be a quickie." Suki assured him. Jeff wore a sour expression. "Oh, come on, Jeff," she rolled her eyes again. "You'll get to fly the plane."

He perked up. "Some consolation. And Marie goes with us."

"Of course," Suki said. "I'll need her to keep me sane."

"We'll keep each other sane," Marie said dryly.

At that moment, Tami and Lew's eyes unglazed. Mac walked back in and to his seat but remained standing. "Josh Jackson's guards allowed him to phone me." He went on to tell them what he had just learned. Josh and Bret wanted to donate their plans for a new device to monitor Earth's rotation, which Mac welcomed, providing instructions on how to submit them. Next, Mac relayed to them the gist of Josh's information on Singleton's hiring Akari to spread stories that aliens were behind Earth's erratic rotation.

The table erupted with a chorus of questions. Mac waved his hands to quiet them. "Singleton insists he no longer wants to work with the aliens because he sees them as a threat to the survival of the planet. He thinks that if enough noise is made, governments will step up their investigations and the official attention will deter the aliens."

"That wouldn't be good for you guys!" Chris exclaimed. "He doesn't know that Akari is a kind of alien herself?"

"Oh no," Mac replied. "He doesn't know we exist. For some crazy reason, Bandela, in his Gabe Jackson persona, told Singleton that he was one of the extraterrestrials."

Consumed by laughter, Jeff managed to speak, "I love it! Did we put the fear in Singleton! Or at least you guys did." He looked at the Synons. "And Chris's spaceship." Jeff sobered. "But Chris is right; we don't want Singleton blabbing about it to the wrong people. Mac, do your government ties stretch enough to squelch any snooping that gets too close to the truth about the Realm?"

"Of course," Mac reassured him. "Also, remember it would be hard for Singleton to tell a coherent story without inadvertently confessing to the kidnapping. I think that might be why he hopes to stay out of it by creating enough clamor that the authorities will find the aliens without his involvement. Now he's trying to find contacts to expedite that. He has no idea that he's asking to align with those he previously met as aliens."

After more laughter from the entire table, Jeff changed the subject. "So what about Josh? Why did he tell you about Singleton's plan? And why did Akari tell Josh?"

Lew answered. "Self-preservation. As Synons, Josh and Akari know their existence depends on Earth remaining healthy, with an abundance of life forms continuously feeding power to the Realm, and by extension to them. They know what's happening there right now. I genuinely think both of them are ready to come to our aid to save themselves."

Jeff scowled. "I hope you're right, Lew."

Mac said, "The island is about ready for Josh and Bret. They won't be kept from using their minds, but they'll be embedded with mental links to strong Earth-Synon guards at all times."

■　　■　　■

Tami had returned to her room to put away the few things she had before fetching Annilu and departing for the Realm. Bandela-Josh Jackson barged into her mind. "How dare you!" she shouted.

"Sorry for the intrusion, but they would only let me make one phone call. I have something crucial to say."

"Go ahead, but be concise."

"I'm being wasted sitting here in jail, and it will continue on that island. Let me go to the Realm. I've built my strength considerably. Bret won't go. He's been here too long. He's ready to help, though."

"You're going to the island." She attempted to break the connection.

Bandela-Josh stubbornly held on. "You know you need me! Haven't I proved my loyalty by allowing you to throw me in this brig and plan to exile me on a remote island?"

She held her mind quiet for a moment as assessments of the situation played deep beyond Bandela's reach. The she replied. "I'll confer with the others and be in touch. Follow MacIntyre's orders." This time her barriers slammed into Bandela, excising his mind from hers.

CHAPTER TWENTY-FOUR

Jeff was filled with dread the day he, Suki, and Marie flew to New York. They were spared the stress of a bustling commercial airport by Jeff piloting them in Mac's small plane to a private airfield. Flying lifted his mood. A YCN car whisked them straight to the studio.

Jeff was surprised to be met by Jack Harvey and News Director Vera Schechner, who ushered them into a dressing room with a well-appointed reception area where they were invited to be seated. Jeff eyed a table laden with food and drink.

Vera laughed. "Ready for lunch? Please help yourselves while we chat a few moments."

"Thank you," Jeff said. All three travelers grabbed plates.

While they munched, Jack ticked off the upcoming process. Jeff was immensely relieved when informed that the interview would not be live. "That doesn't mean you can stop and start or change anything. We're not in the habit of allowing guests to edit their interviews," Vera said. "However, we must sometimes edit for time." A bright smile lit up her face. "I know how proud of all of you my dear friend Bailey MacIntyre must be."

Jeff looked closer at the middle-aged woman. She was attractive; despite her position she seemed to be wearing little or no makeup. Her gray hair was worn in a stylish short cut with bangs touching the top rim of her large glasses. She called Mac a dear friend. Did she know what he was? Jeff recalled Mac's harsh comment about having to put a mission above all else. Had he been thinking about her?

Suki had spoken into Jeff's silence. "We're so grateful for this opportunity. It means a lot to me."

"You've done very well, Suki." Vera turned to Marie. "You and Jeff were close before all this happened, weren't you?"

Marie looked surprised. "Yes. We worked together. And were best friends."

Grinning, Jeff interjected, "It took an upheaval in our lives for us to realize that we were a lot more than best friends. I'd be a mess now if it weren't for Marie. And she's been invaluable to our work. She's a whizz at all things computer: networking; cybersecurity; you name it. Maybe more important, good with people."

Marie blushed. "Don't exaggerate." She offered a mock scowl.

"The strength of your bond will sustain you in the coming days," Vera mused.

Jack glanced at the wall clock. "Well, we better give you a little rest time now. And chow time." He laughed. "Jeff, someone will arrive in a while to help you get ready. Suki can tell you what to expect. Stay relaxed. You're in good hands. See you on set," he said, shaking hands with Jeff.

Vera also rose to leave. "After the interview, Jack and I will go into overdrive preparing for his live show that will air your interview. So we probably won't see you again on this trip. Feel free to hang out here as long as you'd like and watch the live show."

"Thanks so much." As Jeff was about to reach out a hand to her, she approached and kissed his cheek.

"We'll stay in touch," she said.

*　　*　　*

Jack Harvey was a skilled and experienced interviewer. His questions and remarks deftly guided Jeff through the primary points the audience should hear about Confluence. Through his upbringing, college, the Air Force, and work in cybersecurity, Jeff had developed the ability to sharply focus his attention. He called upon that experience as he sat across from Harvey, managing to ignore the cameras, making eye contact with his interviewer, and rapidly reviewing his words before letting them escape his lips.

He was glad of all the practice Suki had made him endure, especially when Harvey inquired about how Jeff had learned he was telepathic. Careful to conceal confidential facts, he had rehearsed this answer until it naturally flowed. "I think it was with me as a child growing up in Cherokee, but I didn't have an experience I could definitely say was telepathic until a little over a year ago when I heard the voice of a person in distress, not with my ears but in my mind. It was like a dream in some ways. We carried on a conversation that led to my being able to get the person help."

"Do you think the urgency of the situation impacted your receptiveness?" Harvey asked.

"Maybe. It's a bit of a complicated story, but it led me and the person I helped to others like us. That's why I encourage anyone who received that Earth image to contact us." He recited the website address that scrolled across the bottom of the screen as he spoke.

Harvey had more questions. "Does Confluence have plans for organizing these new telepaths to help society?"

"Yes, definitely. First they must learn to control and use their ability. They might need counseling to adjust to their new situation. That's our first obligation."

"Are you concerned about negative backlash such as fear and distrust of people like you from those who lack this particular ability?"

"That must be a consideration. People tend to distrust what they don't understand. I've already seen some unfortunate inferences from social media and news outlets, which I won't repeat. In most any group there are a few people who will use anything available to their own personal advantage, often at the expense of others. It's their closest peers who can see any warning signs and find acceptable interventions. Confluence wants to emphasize the far greater good that can result from our working together and with society at large. I should mention that smaller special interest groups are already forming among those who have come forward. They range across many topics. A very popular one concerns the environment and climate change."

Harvey returned to his prior line of questioning. "Even though you downplay the potential for abuse, I can see our viewers out there jumping up and waving their fists at the screen. I'd be remiss not to mention a blaring potential. That's the use of telepathy to invade the minds of others and persuade them to specific viewpoints or actions, or to steal vital information."

Jeff knew that Harvey would have to broach that topic. He detested the need to discuss it at all but knew this was his opportunity to provide logical explanations. He managed a short laugh. "We all love a good what-if. I can give your audience some reassurance. First, a telepath can't easily invade another person's mind, especially those who aren't telepathic. Those of us with the ability can learn to erect barriers that keep out invaders. This is why it's so important to get training and counseling. It's basic etiquette, respecting privacy and the sanctity of our personal thoughts. We can block everyone except those we give permission to contact us. With those people we can set up varying protocols."

Harvey interrupted before Jeff could continue. "That doesn't seem to be what happened when someone broadcast that image. It invaded the minds of thousands of people across the world."

"And I stress that only people who possess telepathic ability were able to receive it. The one who accidentally sent it had no idea what they were doing. It was an impulsive action by someone who happened to be extremely strong telepathically but didn't know it. It's evidence for why we each need to harness our abilities."

Harvey asked a few more questions, then aimed at summarizing the content of the interview. When he finally said they were out of time Jeff had to stop himself from a loud exhale of relief.

Jeff was escorted back to the reception area where Marie and Suki were resting. Marie saw that exhaustion was claiming Jeff and suggested that she and Suki let him nap. After all, they needed him alert to get them home. Suki agreed and gave Marie a tour of the YCN facilities. They stayed to watch the live broadcast of the interview over dinner before heading back to the airfield.

Jeff hated seeing himself on television and was critical of his performance; Suki insisted that he came across like a professional. Marie added, "Your natural warmth came through. I think you did a great job of connecting with the audience as a person just like them."

"I agree," Suki said. "Jeff, you also were excellent at acknowledging touchy subjects and defusing them. I think you accomplished a lot for Confluence tonight."

"I just hope a lot of the ones who've stayed quiet will be encouraged to talk to us now. And that the public won't treat us like dangerous mutants."

■　　■　　■

Thanks to Suki's astute placement, the Confluence message rapidly spread across all forms of media, including Confluence pages she established on social media sites.

Reactions from those who were obviously not telepathic spread across a broad spectrum. The majority of opinions fell into a moderate stance urging open-mindedness while cautioning that some appropriate laws should be quickly passed. There was optimism and pessimism, including a potent strand of Jack Harvey's predicted fear and distrust.

Those who recognized that they were telepaths reacted in varied ways. Many had already reached out for help and training; a few chose to remain silent, hoping they could just ignore their newfound ability. Unfortunately, a small percentage saw it as a windfall for themselves—a means of enrichment by fleecing the gullible. A spate of new ads appeared for psychics, fortune-tellers, and other "mind-reading" services.

The regional Confluence centers saw a brisk increase in applicants. Lana was working with others to streamline the interview and training criteria already in use. Locating those who might be candidates for the special Earth Project was paramount in the screening process. Capable trainers were required for each different language represented as regional groups were formed.

It was a complicated process that was being carried on simultane-ously in the major Confluence centers across the globe.

■   ■   ■

Roger Singleton was livid. How could he, a genius, not be tele-pathic when thousands of ordinary people apparently were? It was absolutely unfair. He fantasized over the money and power he could amass by plucking passwords, account numbers, confi-dential and classified information from the minds of the rich and powerful, many of whom he had, or could easily attain, access to.

Then he saw Jack Harvey interview Jeff Hawke and freaked out. "What th…!" Singleton shouted at his television. "It's that Jeff guy who was with the aliens! He infiltrated my security! He was in my home!"

Singleton's mind raced as he listened to this man calling himself Jeff Hawke speak. He was a telepath! Was he also an alien? What if all these telepaths coming out of the woodwork were actually aliens? They were embedded as humans all over the world! Singleton tried to quiet his mind. He rewound to the beginning of the interview, resolving to focus on Hawke's words and demeanor. Hawke was disgustingly likable and eloquent. Hawke's presentation was designed to elicit sympathy and offer reassurance. These weren't freaks, they were just ordinary people who happened to have an ability everyone else lacked. They would be knights in shining armor. The good mutants. "Ha!" Singleton barked in ridicule.

Now he could point out two prominent "people" who were, or were close to, aliens: Dr. Gabe Jackson and Jeff Hawke. Singleton was in a quandary. His prior resolve to back off from connecting aliens to the telepaths evaporated, yet there was no way he could "out" Hawke without incriminating himself. He had vital information that could lead authorities directly to the alien infiltrators. Should he anonymously report them? No, government investigators were too good at tracking down anyone who tried to hide their trail. Could he demand immunity for providing valuable information? After all, his reason for taking Emma Goodsen was to get to her alien contacts. Didn't the means justify the intended end? He was acting on behalf of humanity.

The widespread seismic activity further alarmed Singleton. The aliens were escalating. He left another message for Akari then made a hefty donation to Confluence through its website, using his own name. Maybe that would get him some attention.

Just as he was about to peruse his contact list, Akari called him. Her first words were, "Did you see that interview?"

"I did." He paused to think, then decided to take a chance. "I know Hawke. He's not what he seems. He's either an alien or an alien collaborator. It leads me to conclude that all these telepaths are the same as him."

Akari knew who Jeff Hawke was, and who his affiliations were. She conveyed only what she needed to. "I've come across him before through Suki Kurosawa. I'm certain that he's human. I think you're wrong about these telepaths."

Singleton was uncomfortable. His people had been unable to maintain adequate surveillance on Akari. Her movements and contacts remained mysterious. She already knew more than he should have allowed, so he might as well continue to take advantage of whatever she could do for him. "Regardless, there's an insidious plot underway that does involve aliens. I think humanity might be in extreme danger. I need to make an immunity deal in exchange for vital information that might also incriminate me in another matter."

Before he could continue with a request for possible contacts Akari interrupted. "I am familiar with a covert government agent who might be just the person. Let me make some inquiries. Meantime, don't take any actions on this matter. I'm relatively certain I can be of assistance."

"Can you give me their name?"

"I prefer not to at the moment, since he might not be the right person. Just be patient."

CHAPTER TWENTY-FIVE

Construction of the new American Confluence center was under way at the camp. The airstrip and small tower were now operational under Mannie Patel's management. Land had been cleared and prepared only enough to allow for the construction of low-rise apartments, offices, and classrooms surrounded by vegetation. Lew and Mac had bought up enough surrounding acreage to accommodate the necessary buildings and leave plenty of undeveloped space, including wide buffer zones shielding the facility from nearby roads. The only inhabitants not actively involved were the three telepathic children. Lana Adams was handling multiple duties, working with the kids, while continuously monitoring and refining protocols for interviewing, accessing, and utilizing the capabilities of new telepaths. Marie continued to work with Asya and others on maintaining the global computer and communications network.

Jeff was kept busy as spokesperson. To better manage his time, he and Suki arranged for requests for him to speak or be interviewed to be done remotely. A small studio with an attractive background and all the necessary equipment was set up.

Jeff was relieved to be able to stay there where he could spend as much time with Marie as they could coordinate.

Although under time pressure, everyone was in good spirits, feeling they were effectively working toward a common objective.

■ ■ ■

Jeff and Marie enjoyed a rare evening at home together. After dinner, as they nestled on the sofa watching a movie Cosmos didn't cuddle with them in his usual way. The sleek black cat was restless. He stalked into the kitchen, and they heard his kitty door swing shut behind him as he went outside. "That's not like him," Marie muttered.

Jeff observed with a grin. "Yeah, he's become like a dog, hanging around with us inside at night."

Marie looked over at Jeff to see his eyes glazed. Was he talking to the cat?

At that moment, she felt a shudder, not just her body, but the sofa on which they sat. "Did you feel that?" She jumped up to see the light over the dining table swing wildly, then she nearly fell over. It was like she stood on the deck of a swaying boat. Marie heard glassware rattling and hoped her vintage pieces had survived.

Jeff was also on his feet, struggling for balance. He reached over and grabbed her. "Earthquake!" The word was spoken into sudden darkness as the power blinked out. "Be careful," Jeff warned. "I hope my phone is still on the table. Ok, I hear it beeping." She could barely see him as he felt for it. "Got it." His face flickered in the screen's white light. He fell back on the sofa. "Sit back down," he ordered, "while I deal with these messages."

She complied. The quake seemed to be over, but she knew that there could be more seismic activity. Jeff was mumbling to himself as he rapidly typed. Marie stayed quiet to not disturb him as she searched for her own phone, but it had fallen off the table in front of the sofa. She gently felt around with a foot until she located it. There were emergency alert messages and texts from several people, among them Lana assuring her that the kids were fine but upset at what had happened to Earth.

Marie's thoughts went to Cosmos. She carefully rose and made her way to the back door where he had exited. She opened it to darkness and a brisk wind under a starless sky. She began calling the cat, wishing she could talk mentally to him. Suddenly Jeff was behind her pulling her back inside. "Stay in a safe place! There can be aftershocks that are worse than the initial event."

"I'm worried about Cosmos," she whispered.

"So am I," Jeff replied. "I can't reach his mind. That doesn't mean he's not all right. He might just have closed it for self-protection." That didn't seem reasonable to Marie, but she didn't say anything else about it.

"Let's go back to the couch," Jeff's encircling arm guided her. "There's nothing immediately around it that could fall on us."

"Except the ceiling," she said sarcastically. "Did you learn anything?"

"Everyone at the camp is okay. We'll have to wait 'til daylight to see about things, especially the stuff under construction. It didn't seem too bad. I don't think there was any real damage in the house," he said.

"I want to check on my vintage glassware. There was a lot of rattling."

"We have to wait." They reached the sofa and gingerly sat down. Both started looking at their phones again. "Lew says emergency power generators kicked in at the Tech Center. No equipment damage apparent yet. Cell tower's still standing, obviously." He chuckled.

"Can you ask Lew to reach out to Cosmos?"

"I want to, but he's way too busy. We'll just have to keep sending love to our kitty and trust that he'll be all right."

She felt a tear slide down her face.

*　*　*

Not uncommon, earthquakes in the mountains were usually localized and short-lived. This one did not follow precedent. Effects were felt all over western and Piedmont North Carolina, eastern Tennessee, and Northeast Georgia. Multiple aftershocks occurred, some lasting far longer than the initial quake. Daylight revealed considerable damage across the three-state area. Far more concerning were reports of similar quakes on almost every continent. Some were stronger, causing more damage, especially in areas where buildings weren't constructed to withstand them.

In one such place, located in sub-Saharan Africa, a young woman named Zora was asleep next to her husband of six months in the house that had recently been built for them. They lived in a small farming community where the people were proud of their heritage and clung to traditional ways. Zora woke abruptly to find herself covered in something. She screamed, floundering to push away the material under which she was buried. Although it was dark, she felt around and found that she was lying on the floor. She had apparently fallen or been thrown from their bed and portions of the ceiling had fallen on her.

Her screams brought no response from her husband. She called out to him to be met only with silence. An acrid smell permeated the room. Zora realized it was smoke. Flames flickered beyond what was left of her home's walls. She pushed away the material over her and jumped to her feet. The flames brought enough illumination into the small room for her to carefully make her way through the debris-strewn floor to the other side of the bed. She stumbled on something and nearly fell. A shriek escaped as she realized that it was her husband's body lying on the floor, crushed under a tall wooden cabinet that had stood on the wall near the bed. As she tried to find a way out of the debris she heard a distinct voice, but she couldn't understand what it said. It seemed to be coming from inside her head rather than outside the house. "Who are you?" she screamed.

The voice spoke again, this time in her own language. "I'm Asya. I want to help you. What has happened?"

"Where are you? I don't see you!" Zora cried.

"Did you recently have a vision of the Earth in the sky?"

"How do you know about that?" Zora was in a panic, shock about to claim her reasoning.

"I, and many others, saw it too. It led to understanding that we have an ability to talk to each other through our minds like we're doing now. I'm in Turkey but know your language and that you're in Africa."

"Oh," Zora said woodenly. She was beginning to feel numb, like she was living in a dream.

"Do you have a mobile phone?"

"Yes."

"Good. Can you find your mobile?"

Zora had left it on the table next to her bed. It was covered in debris but worked. "It's okay. What do you want me to do with it?"

"Just leave it on; our electronics can locate its signal and find you. Tell me exactly where you are as best you can."

"I have to get outside. There's a fire. People are running and shouting."

"Go ahead! Take the phone. Just think what you want to say to me, that's faster than talking. Let me know what the conditions are around you."

When she got outside, Zora saw that most of the nearby homes had been toppled along with power poles. Flames shot from several houses that were next to the forest that also burned. Her neighbors were frantically digging at the ruins of several homes. They shouted for her to help; people were buried. Zora gave Asya her location then joined the rescue effort.

After a short time, Zora heard Asya's voice, "Help is coming. Watch for helicopters. They'll shine bright lights on the ground looking for a place to land. Any time you want to talk to me, just think my name and I'll respond."

■　■　■

Similar events occurred around the world. Earthquake victims who knew they were telepathic reached out. Some were even buried under rubble. Confluence members in or close to quake locations searched with open minds for other telepaths who might need help. Others who were unaware of their ability had experiences similar to Zora's.

The news media gradually began to share stories of how Confluence was demonstrating the organizational effectiveness it had built. Its ability to get information on specific places in need to local and international aid groups saved lives and facilitated the start of efforts to help survivors. These were the kind of human-interest stories journalists loved presenting. The positive face of telepathy was highlighted as individuals were interviewed on camera relating the amazing stories of helpful strangers' voices in their heads and the short time it took for aid to arrive because of them.

■   ■   ■

Everyone at the new North American headquarters on the site of the former Unique camp was engaged in efforts to assess and mitigate damage in the areas in which they worked.

Marie had to put Cosmos out of her mind and focus on the international communications grid that was being strained to its limit.

Reports were arriving from Confluence centers relating the extent of damage or injuries, or the good news that they were okay. One report was stunning and vital enough for immediate relay to MacIntyre. Above active tectonic plate boundaries, the island on which Bandela and Bret were soon to be transported had been nearly obliterated. The several people working there were missing, presumed to have been washed away by the sea's inundation that left water covering what had not sunk into the gaping Earth beneath it. All structures were destroyed.

"Earth has spoken," Tami declared. "I'll depart right away to assess the situation in the Realm and confer with Tork. We must be in close proximity to confer on such a vital matter. However, I believe Bandela must soon join us there. Can you keep him where he is a bit longer?"

"He has little choice," Mac replied.

Mac had been vehemently opposed to Josh's request to return to the Realm and help. He had bellowed, "Of course he's strong! He's plundered every iota of power he could from the Earth and its inhabitants!"

Lew had pointed out that Josh-Bandela's strength was being wasted and would not yield value on the island comparable to the resources required to keep him secure there.

Jeff had countered that the power Tork would have to expend guarding him in the Realm could be greater than what Bandela contributed.

Each had made valid points. Mac had declared that Josh would stew a little longer. Now it appeared that Earth had made the decision for them.

CHAPTER TWENTY-SIX

Dealing with the quake aftermath required MacIntyre's full attention. He was conferring with Chris and the architect on modifications to strengthen their structures' earthquake protection when he got a call from Confluence's accounting manager. He answered with a customary line, "This better be important!"

"I think you should know someone named Roger Singleton, located in Sarasota, Florida, has just made a whopping donation to Confluence. That name and location rang a bell with me from last year's activity."

MacIntyre recalled the recent message from Josh. What was Singleton up to? He was obviously trying to get their attention. "You were right to alert me. Thank you." He disconnected.

That evening, in exhaustion, everyone took a break, retiring to their respective dwellings, some of which still needed cleanup or restoration. The rambling farmhouse had fared surprisingly well. Since its purpose was to offer refuge to Synons, the house was furnished only enough to give a lived-in appearance to visiting humans. Nevertheless, the two longtime personas had grown comfortable with the kind of cozy atmosphere people favored. They sat in battered old recliners in the parlor whose walls were lined with book-filled shelves.

Mac told Lew about the recent communications regarding Singleton. Lew chuckled. "He's spooked. He really believes extra-terrestrials are behind everything."

"His meddling makes him more dangerous than ever. We need to rein him in. I'd like to know what he has to tell us. I'm almost certain he thinks he can be absolved of a kidnapping charge by offering identities of aliens, probably Jeff and Gabe Jackson."

"Of course," Lew nodded. "He would have recognized Jeff on television, and Jackson told Singleton he was an alien."

Mac sat pondering for a long while. "Akari says he's terrified by the rapid changes in climate and geological activity. He still thinks aliens are involved and is ready to lend his capabilities to whoever can best help manage it. Akari has convinced him that's us."

"She's always been a double agent, but I suppose she's as ready to turn for her own survival as Singleton is."

Mac agreed. "More than Singleton, she knows the true stakes."

Lew stroked his chin. "I don't like that Singleton got away with kidnapping a child."

Mac's bushy eyebrows knit. "If he's truly afraid, we can manipulate him. We should intimidate him and demand he stop spreading rumors. Let's think about maybe letting him come to us with what he thinks is valuable information, then turn the tables somehow."

"Somehow," Lew drawled. "We need to think like devious people."

∎   ∎   ∎

Singleton was amazed when told he would be taken by private plane to the Bahamas Confluence center. He struggled to control his thoughts, wary of the several other passengers who turned out to be telepaths on their way to work there. He distrusted their insistence that they couldn't invade an unwilling mind. Nevertheless, the passengers congenially chatted and tried to bring Singleton into the conversation. Aware that he had to learn to be courteous to the mutants, he offered brief replies to their questions.

Singleton was taken to a different area than the other passengers and ushered into a small waiting room. Now he was nervous for a new reason. He had absolutely no idea what awaited him. U.S. Marshalls could swarm in and take him into custody. The door opened; a tall, middle-aged man with shoulder-length graying hair and bushy eyebrows invited him in. Like Singleton, he wore business attire. The small office was sparsely furnished with a desk facing a guest chair.

"I'm Bailey MacIntyre." He shook Singleton's hand and asked him to be seated.

Not giving the other man a chance to speak, Singleton attempted to hide his jitters with bravado. "I'm eager to offer my considerable management expertise to your organization, but I had hoped to speak with government officials who could take advantage of vital information I have."

"I'm affiliated with both Confluence and the government. What do you have?"

Singleton was outraged. "This is a highly confidential national security matter!"

MacIntyre produced a National Security Agency badge. "My clearance is as high as it goes."

Trying to cover his astonishment, Singleton smiled slyly. "Oh, I see. The government is wisely monitoring this new organization."

"Nothing warrants that. I'm volunteering as a management consultant for Confluence."

"Exactly the role I propose for myself. I have extensive experience." He smiled smugly. "And the wealth to prove it."

Not responding, MacIntyre gazed intently at Singleton.

Resisting the urge to divert his eyes, Singleton demurred. "Of course we can discuss that later. I'm now comfortable sharing what I know with you. Prepare to be shocked."

"Continue."

"I can attest to the identity of two extraterrestrial entities who are posing as men right here on Earth." Singleton sat back, waiting for the shock to set in.

MacIntyre's expression remained blank. "I suppose you plan to name Dr. Gabe Jackson and Jeff Hawke."

Singleton gasped. He experienced an impulse to bolt for the door, but was frozen to his chair.

When MacIntyre picked up a hefty file, a terrified Singleton exclaimed, "What is that?"

"The FBI file on you."

He waved his hand dismissively. "Of course they have a file on me. It's standard procedure. I've provided countless valuable patents to the government, especially the Defense Department."

"This isn't on your business. It's about kidnapping charges."

He had walked into a trap. Singleton was struggling to keep up his façade. "Who the hell are you, really?"

"Just who I say I am. I consulted with a multi-agency task force investigating the kidnapping of then-five-year-old Emma Goodsen."

The façade crumbled. Singleton slumped. Then he summoned his survival instinct. "Ha. I invited that kid to visit with me in Florida. She was all too happy to accompany me."

"A five-year-old can't legally make a decision like that. Plus, we have the woman you hired to abduct the child. Would you like to see her deposition?"

"So why didn't you arrest me? Is it because you wanted to let the kid lead me to her alien friends?"

"We wanted to nail the people who were posing as aliens."

"Jeff Hawke? These mutants?" Singleton sat back, his mind working again.

"Jeff Hawke was part of an elaborate sting operation utilizing holograms and a fake spacecraft lent to us by a film production company. We're still looking for those who have been extorting people by pretending to be aliens and threatening them. It appears that mental breakdowns and at least one suicide can be attributed to their cons."

"Still you didn't arrest me? What else is going on?"

MacIntyre didn't blink an eye. "The parents didn't want to put their traumatized child through the trial process. They decided not to press charges right then. We do have a deposition." He turned his laptop to face Singleton. A video of Emma Goodsen was paused on its screen. MacIntyre pressed the play button. A male voice off-screen asked, "Is this a picture of the man who held you in his home?" A hand appeared giving Emma a photograph.

"Yes, that's the mean man!" Emma's voice shook.

"Please show the camera the picture, Emma." She turned the photo and held it next to her face so that both were visible and identifiable. It was a photo of Singleton.

"Did he hurt you?"

Emma's face scrunched up "He yelled at me, and jerked me, and tried to hit me. The lady stopped him, but she was bad too. She stuck needles in my arm. It hurt."

MacIntyre turned the laptop back around and stopped the video. "There's more."

"What do you want?" Singleton snapped.

"Cease and desist all activity linking extraterrestrials to telepaths, Earth's erratic rotation, climate change, or anything else. Stop talking about aliens entirely."

Singleton knew he was onto something. "Aha! I'm getting too close to the truth about aliens! I knew it. You want to keep it quiet to prevent panic. You have no way to counter them."

Mac's expression had never changed. His face remained impassive. "I'm not at liberty to discuss anything about potential extraterrestrial activity on Earth. I'll say no more, except to warn you not to keep spreading disinformation."

Singleton asked smugly, "So what about Dr. Jackson?"

For the first time, MacIntyre's expression changed. He laughed loudly. "That kook? He's ruined his career with crazy stories and stunts like he pulled with you. He's no more an alien than you are."

Singleton's scalp tingled. "What do you know about his interactions with me? And how?"

MacIntyre laughed again. "He's a loose cannon, and since he has provided sensitive information and devices to the government, his behavior warrants surveillance. We know he visited your mountain facility. He must have given you reason to see him as an alien, if he didn't claim outright that he was one."

Singleton was troubled that the government had discovered his covert facility. Now they would probably monitor it. He tried to be nonchalant. "I sort of suspected as much, but brilliant men are often eccentric. His knowledge and extraordinary robotics plans led me to believe his assertion that he was alien. I should have been more skeptical, but I was, and still am, concerned about extraterrestrial activity here. I've studied it closely for a long time." He paused, then he couldn't help but taunt. "So that's all? That's all I have to do to avoid being indicted?"

"No. You'll do no more business with the federal government."

Singleton blanched. He had just lost a vast amount of his ongoing income.

MacIntyre continued, "There's a kidnapping indictment in this file. At present, there are reasons it is not being acted upon. However, your passport has been revoked because the warrant is pending. I repeat. Pending. Do not consider getting revenge in any way, including defaming Confluence. You exist on the edge of a precipice. Don't misstep."

Stunned, Singleton struggled to regain a toehold. "I understand, but must convey how truly remorseful I am. I only acted in the interest of humanity. Could I gift my design for a cyborg to the government? Whether through alien action or climate and geological degradation, we could soon be faced with unlivable conditions."

MacIntyre stared at him. "I can't imagine the funding, technology and expertise will exist in the near future to utilize such a thing. We need more immediate assistance. We've recently received plans for an advanced system for more precise monitoring of Earth's rotation. Perhaps you could utilize your manufacturing capabilities to produce and distribute it to designated facilities."

"Of course! That will at least be some small contribution I can make. Is there nothing more I can do for this Confluence organization?"

"Not at present. We appreciate your generous donation, of course."

Singleton had been on the verge of demanding a refund but decided any placating gesture would benefit him. He smiled and nodded, as his mind calculated the immense financial loss he faced.

MacIntyre stood. "Now, you'll be returned to your home. We'll be in touch regarding the monitoring system."

Stunned, Singleton's mind was numb. He was on a short leash, facing potential imprisonment. His life had changed forever.

CHAPTER TWENTY-SEVEN

The quakes had motivated telepaths around the world to think about new ways in which their unique talent could be used for good.

While training new telepaths, Judilay prompted the formation of a group call the Earth Project, based on the informal name that was being used by Confluence's established human and Synon participants. Those attracted to the group tended to be egalitarian; without undue leadership competition, they smoothly established chapters across the globe. Groups were formed to learn about specific issues and develop plans that could be implemented as quickly as possible.

Their aim was not only to use their unique ability, but to reach out to their own regions with accurate information and calls for everyone to join their effort. They worked at community levels to build enthusiasm and garner workers, energized by the enthusiasm they discovered across demographics. A groundswell rose that facilitated connecting local groups into the national and international Earth Project. Rallies were held across the world. Celebrities lent support and funding, appearing at rallies. Petitions were delivered to lawmakers and corporate leaders, demonstrating their power as voters and consumers. Accurate information on the detrimental effects of climate change, ecosystem destruction, and human mitigation efforts contributed to positive stories. Positive results appeared at a slow but steady pace.

■　　■　　■

Those at the former Tech Center and Unique camp were encouraged by the way that a global network was swiftly growing. They were motivated to complete the North American Confluence Center ahead of schedule, despite the delays caused by the earthquake. That event was a reminder to ensure that the facility was able to withstand the varying types of natural disasters the future could bring. Everyone continued their jobs with renewed vigor and purpose.

The three children summoned the courage to confront MacIntyre.

Emma demanded, "There must be hundreds of telepaths identified in America by now. Why have none been sent here?"

MacIntyre wore a slight smile as he gazed at them. "You kids are tough. You decided to gang up on me without having Jeff or Lana around. Have you discussed this with them?"

Rick answered, "They don't know. Jeff says things have happened so fast, and the earthquake cut into our preparations on the camp."

Mac nodded. "Both true. However, we Synons involved here have made a decision not yet shared with Jeff and Lana. We decided that you three and Jeff will focus solely on the Earth Project. We don't want to dilute your focus by having you train those not suitable for that task. Training has already begun in several stateside locations. When ready, suitable instructors and new students will come here.

"Judilay is preparing a telepath to assume control of the Bahamas Center. You'll be happy to learn that he will then return here as general manager. He's shown real talent for organization and coordination. Coupled with his interpersonal skills, he's an excellent manager. He strongly believes that humans should take over Confluence, but we persuaded him that, at least until the Earth Project reaches some kind of conclusion, he's needed here in that capacity."

The children were elated at the news. "Does Lana know?" Emma inquired.

"Not yet. Judilay will be the one to tell her," Mac gave them a rare smile.

* * *

"I learned so much from Bandela." The eighteenth-century persona of a French royal lady waved a delicate fan. She just managed to perch on the ornately carved and upholstered chair in a dress with a large, bell-shaped skirt. Her hair was piled high, powdered white, and bore varied elaborate decorative items, ranging from flowers to birds.

"You've marvelously recreated this tableau." Her companion wore a male persona of the same period, also elaborately dressed. He crossed his legs, displaying white stockings and pointed-toe shoes. They sat in a formal garden at a cloth-covered table laden with delicacies that included ceramic bowls of fruit balanced on graceful pedestals decorated with rose buds, platters of venison, and decanters of wine.

"I truly miss Bandela," she murmured, fluttering her fan.

"Wine?" he lifted a jeweled decanter.

"Of course," Just as he was pouring, the garden and their own personas began to waver and fade.

"Apparently you didn't learn well enough from him," the gentleman sneered.

"She learned all too well!" Tork's voice shouted in their minds as the entire scene evaporated, along with the elaborately attired personas.

The essences of two weak Synons cowered, sputtering excuses, in the presence of the Realm's acting leader. "I was telling him about Bandela's vivid recreations of his times on Earth and realized the only way to really convey it was to put him into the experience as Bandela had with us here in the Realm."

"There's no justification for squandering our dwindling power with such a blatant mockery of the Realm's struggle for its very existence! How could you be so ignorant?"

The former male courtier pleaded, "If we are to disappear, perhaps we should do so reliving our past glory."

"Those are not the humans to glorify! Didn't Bandela relate any of their history? As Archivist, it was his duty to put the content of his stories into context. While those two you emulated gorged on delicacies, the peasants were starving."

"No," she admitted. "Bandela just put us into the experience he had enjoyed."

"Hopefully you'll have opportunity to learn about how the planet we are charged with protecting got to its current perilous stage. Right now you must join us in our efforts to conserve our power and assist those working on Earth."

■　■　■

Tork ordered all nonessential simulations in the Realm dismantled, but a few were left intact, their inhabitants flagrantly disregarding orders. For the most part, gone were the plethora of elaborate and complex replicas of multiple Earth settings in which resident Synons practiced being human, often enjoying the pleasures of a material world more than learning to nourish human connection to The Living World.

Now they had to relinquish their individual personas and coalesce as the linked species they naturally were. Tork was seeing the mistakes that had been made in small, unnoticed steps across eons. As individual strands of Synon consciousness had been sent to Earth, they had become enticed by many of the very human traits their presence was meant to mitigate. They had been corrupted to the extent that their link to The Living World diminished in proportion to humanity's detachment from Nature. Now when Earth needed their strength the most, it had been squandered.

Instead of rapidly transforming their creations back into ambient energy, the Synons threw good-bye parties. The splendors of ancient Mesopotamia, China, Indus Valley, Mesoamerica, Africa, Greece, Rome, and other civilizations, moving forward in time, had transformed the Realm into a virtual theme park where inhabitants could stroll among pyramids, the Forbidden City, Renaissance palaces, the extraordinary walled Timbuktu, and Middle Eastern casbahs overflowing with luxurious goods, then jump to magnificent modern cities like Singapore, New York, Paris, and Dubai.

As these festivities drained the Realm's dwindling power, Tork sent another urgent plea to Earth for assistance. He was astonished when a tap at his mind signaled that Bandela wished to speak with him. Tork considered rebuffing the renegade but was too curious to do so. He reluctantly allowed the transmission. Bandela poured out his tale, beginning with an assertion that he had been selected by Earth or The Living World itself to experience what the fragile planet faced. He took it as a sign that he should dedicate himself to preventing that future. Then he related how his overtures had been rejected; now he languished in prison while his enormous strength could be used to replenish the Realm.

Tork listened with uncharacteristic patience. The Realm desperately needed strong Synons who could motivate its residents to abandon their frivolity that masked despair and unite to save their home. However, when Bandela had resided there he had been weak, ineffective, and uncooperative. On Earth, he had become a renegade leader. Could he repurpose those qualities for a beneficial outcome for all rather than just himself?

He addressed Bandela brusquely, "I hope you haven't just wasted my time. I will take up your request with others. You'll hear from me."

"That's what TuMa'Aye Gra'Vay recently told me. She seemed amenable to my request, but MacIntyre appears to disapprove."

"I will confer with them. Please be patient." Tork closed his mind.

■ ■ ■

TuMa'Aye Gra'Vay and Annilu returned to a fading Realm. Its previously consistent rainbow glow was now only a dull, grayish glimmer. The Realm appeared to be suffering from Earth's distress more than the planet herself. Certainly more than her apathetic dominant race.

Annilu was still bitter at having been ordered away from Earth, but was stunned by the change she saw in the Realm. "What can we do?" she exclaimed. TuMa'Aye Gra'Vay had never witnessed her so upset. Humans had left some effect on her after all. TuMa'Aye reminded Annilu to conserve power in order to direct it toward strengthening the Realm.

Tork greeted them effusively, then lapsed into an anxious litany of disasters they were encountering. He was certainly not demonstrating the directive TuMa'Aye had just given her acolyte. She tried to soothe Tork's stressed mind, only to have her attempt brushed off. "If you'd been here all this time, you'd be as upset as I am!" he chided. "Are there others coming?"

"I've broadcast a plea to all Earth-Synons. The new telepaths are starting to take control of Confluence. That will free up many Earth-Synons to join us here. Ours is a joint mission. Both must succeed." She took in the sparse population of Synons aimlessly floating around. "Let's gather all those here to combine efforts."

Annilu interjected indignantly, "Why hasn't that already been done?"

Tork's retort oozed stronger indignation. "You don't think I've been attempting just that? Your impertinence displays ignorance. Since you spent most of your existence in hibernation, you have no notion of the diminished Synon unity that has resulted from so much time spent among humans. Go ahead and try to round them up!"

Tami Graves's personality emerged in TuMa'Aye's quip, "People call it trying to herd cats."

"I don't understand," Annilu said.

As TuMa'Aye was about to respond, her awareness dimmed. She seemed to be disintegrating. It took all her focus and strength to hold herself together. When she again felt cohesion TuMa'Aye assessed her surroundings. The Realm's essence displayed dark slits that looked like rips in fabric. Next to her, Tork's mighty being held fast to that of Annilu that, like the others surrounding them, wavered, blinking in and out. TuMa'Aye broadcast an order for all entities to join together, assuring them that they could retain their individual strand of identity in the process. Sensing reluctance, she sent a stronger message. "Join or risk destruction!"

A weak but petulant resistance persisted. "We can't be destroyed!"

Tork's voice reverberated, "You can't survive if the Realm doesn't. Unify now!"

The separate thin balls of energy slowly moved to touch one another.

CHAPTER TWENTY-EIGHT

Enthusiasm eluded Jeff and Marie as they tried to concentrate on their tasks. There had been no sign of Cosmos. Every day and night they spent what time they could spare to search near and far. Even though there was little traffic, outside the compound's land locals familiar with the roads sometimes drove fast, so they searched along roadsides. Jeff and Lew scoured the forests for signs of the cat who had found Jeff the night Bandela was captured in the park where the homeless feline had met and befriended TuMa'Aye Gra'Vay. No trace of Cosmos was found.

Jeff was becoming distraught by an empty spot in his mind where he had grown accustomed to the presence of the cat that provided the subliminal comfort of a mental purr. The absence of any trace of the feline's mind dredged up thoughts Jeff couldn't allow to take shape.

■　■　■

Emma enlisted everyone she could to join in search parties, asking those who were telepathic to mentally call for Cosmos.

One day she and the other two kids were testing how far their minds could reach. Suddenly, a torrent of awareness poured through Emma. She heard no voice like when telepathing with her companions or Synons. It was similar to the nonverbal link she had experienced with Cosmos and her own cat Fuzzy, but this was amplified to the point that she grabbed her head with both hands and exclaimed. "Something strong's got into my mind!" Tina and Rick gaped at her in alarm.

Emma sank to the ground, eyes closed, trying to identify the presence. Somehow, she knew that whatever she was in contact with meant her no harm. "Can you back off a bit?" she implored. "You're overwhelming me." Emma blocked Tina and Rick as they sat nearby intently observing her. Her awareness channeled only what her mind perceived. Gradually, the clamor diminished enough that she was able to recognize that more than one distinctly nonverbal mind was linked to hers. Images floated before her mind's eye: the woods, but from strange perspectives, mostly trees looming large and distorted; some forest viewpoints were obviously from within brush and through the tree canopy. At the peripheral sat three children.

Animals! Emma was looking through the eyes of forest creatures! She felt the recognition of loss answering her search for Cosmos. Emma's eyes opened wide; she looked in all directions seeking a glimpse of her mental companions. Just beyond the tree line a squirrel hopped away. She felt a tinge of fear and disconnect. She knew her language and mode of thinking would not be comprehended but hoped the content of the thoughts would somehow transfer. "I'm your friend," her mind pleaded. "Don't leave." The squirrel turned, stood on its hind legs and stared at her. "Hello," Emma sent love to the confused creature. "Thank you for your concern. If you find my friend Cosmos please show me where he is." She transmitted images of the sleek black cat, knowing that to animals like squirrels and birds this represented a dangerous predator to be avoided. Nevertheless, she expanded her message to encompass the expanse of minds that still hovered in hers, trying to stress her sense of loss and the link she shared with this particular feline. Something like a sense of affirmation flowed through her. They would help. She sent the news to Jeff.

▪   ▪   ▪

Jeff was pleased by Emma's ability to communicate with multiple animals at once. Perhaps there were others like her who could help their species learn to treat their fellow creatures with more empathy, understanding, and care.

One day when his schedule was relatively light, Jeff took a much-needed walk into the woods alone, hoping to clear his mind and simply enjoy Nature. The forest surrounding the camp had fallen victim to one of the warmest and driest summers on record, delaying the outburst of early autumn color expected by that date at their altitude. Winds were stripping away those leaves that had lost their green. Instead of the serenity he expected, Jeff was met with a vague sense of foreboding.

Jeff strolled on, pushing thoughts from his mind, striving for the peace he usually felt there. He needed to elevate his mood before going home to Marie for the evening. A cool blast of wind whipped around him. He scanned the sky for rain clouds that weren't there.

He found himself moving toward the spot where the confluence formed. If any place would offer solace, that would be it. He quickened his steps as the breeze picked up.

Gone were the colorful flowers that had surrounded the creek. His feet crunched on brittle dead vegetation.

As Jeff approached the creek, a sliver of familiar presence grazed his mind. The long branches overhanging the small waterfall were still laden, casting deep shade that added shadows to the light that was diminishing as the sun dropped behind mountains. Jeff heard no tinkling music made by the water; its flow was now only a trickle. As he neared, the presence grew. Something lay across the low rock bridge that formed the brink of the confluence that two upper streams toppled over to form one wide creek.

His feet splashed through the shallow water. A dark thing took shape. It was Cosmos, lying face down, all four legs spread out in front of and behind him, chin resting on the rock with water trickling under it. His eyes were closed.

"Cosmos!" Tears sprang to Jeff's eyes as he reached out to touch the black fur. It was warm. He placed his hand in front of the cat's nose and felt breath. He was alive! "Cosmos!" he called out again, but the animal didn't stir. When Jeff reached to gently lift the cat into his arms, he felt resistance. Cosmos hunkered down. He didn't want to be picked up. Jeff forced himself to stay calm. The sliver of presence was still in his mind; Cosmos wasn't totally cut off from him. He gently probed, but the familiar feline mind opened no further. Jeff sensed that Cosmos was preoccupied. All concentration seemed focused on one thing. What?

A new awareness brushed Jeff's mind. It was distant and weak, but recognizable to him. Earth! His body tingled. The impression he received was "I need Cosmos."

How was a little cat able to help Earth? And how long had he been here? How had he survived? Another impression floated into his awareness. It was Cosmos relaying concepts to him. TuMa'Aye Gra'Vay had instructed the cat to take care of Earth while she was in the Realm. There was assurance that Cosmos would be cared for. Jeff was astounded. Had TuMa'Aye Gra'Vay managed to keep Cosmos alive all this time? Jeff addressed Cosmos in the manner to which both were accustomed: Jeff spoke mentally in English, thinking of the meanings behind the words and the accompanying feelings. "Have you been here at the confluence for all these days?" Then another thought hit him. "We looked here and didn't see you." He sent the confusion and wonder he felt. As he spoke, Jeff had gently lifted Cosmos into his arms; this time the cat yielded, pressing himself against Jeff's body.

There was a distinct response. Jeff was amazed at the way it addressed his queries through sharing what he realized was what Cosmos had experienced. Jeff felt a sense of purpose overcoming fear. The Earth shaking. The security of low brush growing next to the river. Darkness. Then he was at the confluence, lying in the shallow water, feeling Earth moving beneath him. Blankness. Small fish appearing in the water within his reach. More blankness. People coming. Conflicting urges. People he loved coming. It wasn't time to go to them. The forest. Hiding as only a feline can.

Jeff felt drained. He moved to the bank and sank onto the ground, holding tightly to the warm bundle in his arms. Jeff sent gratitude to Cosmos and to Earth. She had allowed him to pick up the cat and communicate with him. It must be all right now for him to take Cosmos home. He queried Earth and felt a release.

Wanting to reassure Earth, he sent her thoughts of many telepaths, the Uniques she had asked for to help her survive, adding "We have found many of those you asked us to. They are rallying to your aid."

Her response was shocking. She was definitely rejecting the notion that Unique telepaths were the "they" to which she always had referred. A distinct sense of species identification permeated his mind. He tried to isolate it. The globe, like he had seen it when astral traveling. Humans. All of them. Earth needed all of humanity to help her! His heart sank. How long had some people been trying to do that exact thing? More and more were joining the movement, but there were many people who would never give up their short-sighted priorities and stubborn refusal to consider and learn about ideas with which they disagreed.

How could he answer her? He could only say the truth. "We'll work to unite everyone. We'll do everything we can. Some will not agree." Did she wonder how it was that all species would not want her to survive? Did she have a mind that worked that way? Probably not. Jeff sat for long moments, stroking the purring cat and sending loving and supportive feeling and thought to Earth.

That's all they need to do, he thought. As many as we can get to just feel support, gratitude, and love for the Earth that makes their lives possible, and do what each can to help.

"Will you be all right if I take Cosmos home now?" Jeff inquired. A renewed sense of release came to him. "Thank you. Please reach out if you sense that you are becoming unable to maintain your systems. We will be here for you." He hoped she couldn't sense the feeling that followed his last statement. What could they possibly do to help her if she was losing control?

The wind had become stronger and colder. The shadows deepened with the addition of dark clouds. "Let's get going, Cosmos. I think we might have a rainstorm!"

Before he got back to the camp large drops of water were pelting them. Ignoring people he passed who called out in surprise as they saw him running with the cat in his arms, Jeff dashed to his truck. Once inside, he deposited Cosmos on the passenger seat and texted Marie and Emma. "Okay, boy. We're going home."

CHAPTER TWENTY-NINE

Annilu was somewhat appeased by TuMa'Aye Gra'Vay's confidence in her ability when she announced that the two of them would be escorting Bandela to the Realm. Accompanying them were two other Earth-Synons. Together, the four surrounded Bandela's essence and herded it through a Passageway.

Upon arrival in the Realm, all four were stunned at the degree to which it had literally shrunk. Tork was desperately attempting to gather the wisps of individual Synons listlessly floating around. His need was so urgent that he was even glad to see Bandela.

The renegade addressed Tork, "Please believe that I am sincerely dedicated to saving the Realm and the planet to which it's tethered. I recognize that is the only way for me to survive."

Tork glowered. "So you continue to be driven solely by selfish impulses."

"No. No! I misspoke. Of course I want to survive; however, emulating the worst of human traits for so long has taken a toll on me. I'm weary of the constant strife of interacting with them. My innate Synon sensibilities and instincts have been revived; I now see the overall picture and what must be done."

Tork snorted. "Your slimy attempts to placate me have no effect. However, I will offer you an opportunity to prove your sincerity. You are a Synon with much experience and knowledge that can be of value in this crisis."

"Thank you. I am prepared to apply my abilities to persuading those here to abandon their decadent lifestyles. As the humans say, it takes one to know one."

Tork regarded Annilu and the other two guards. "Monitor him closely. Don't allow him to shut you out of his mind. You'll be disgusted by what you encounter and must remain silent. Don't react to things Bandela or others think, say or do. Let him play out his tactics." His attention turned to TuMa'Aye Gra'Vay. "Are you comfortable sending him off with these three as guardians? Your help is needed elsewhere."

"I have complete confidence in them." She addressed Annilu, "Nevertheless, I'd like to keep a sliver of awareness within your mind to be aware of what you're witnessing. If needed, I'll be there with assistance immediately."

Annilu's mental tone was curt. "Of course. I appreciate your confidence."

■   ■   ■

Bandela didn't need directions to the revelers; their flagrant activity was a beacon. Flanked by his guards, Bandela drifted through the dim essence of the Realm past bright, noisy vignettes that were like visions from the window of a moving vehicle. They were persistent enough to activate replicated sensory perception in the four Synons despite their not being in human personas. They arrived at a large display that elicited gasps.

Before them lay the Palace of Versailles, its formal gardens and fountains spread out before and around it. Annilu was incensed at the blatant squandering of power but stifled a reaction. Bandela moved toward the music drifting from within the expansive structure. They found themselves in an immense hall of gold and crystal with tall mirrors lining walls illuminated by hundreds of candles in glittering jeweled sconces. The room twirled with vibrant colors adorning people attired in the most opulent of late seventeenth-century French fashion. Ladies in wide bell-shaped skirts and ornately decorated hair piled high danced with men crowned with long, often curled hair or wigs and dressed in long coats of rich fabric, stockings and fancy shoes. A cloying scent of perfume hung in the air.

Bandela headed right for the couple dancing in the middle of the crowd that had left a circle of space around them. Annilu was thrown off guard when Bandela abruptly appeared above the couple in the form of a huge, scaled dragon exhaling flames. The dancers were so stunned that many personas disappeared, replaced by floundering knots of energy. The two impersonating King Louis XVI and his queen Marie Antoinette glared defiantly at the hovering specter. "Remove yourself at once!" Louis demanded. "I did not order your appearance!"

Annilu and her two companions had quickly regained composure and moved to surround the dragon that was far larger than them. An order flashed from Annilu, and the three guards materialized as one new dragon so big it loomed over Bandela and the entire hall. Only the high, curved ceiling provided sufficient room for the new creature.

Utilizing the terrifying Synon command voice, Bandela sent sound waves reverberating through the structure, causing it to waver. "Cease this abomination or be dissolved!"

The remaining personas began to dissipate. Only Louis and Marie Antionette remained steadfast. "You have no authority over us! And we all know you can never act on your threat. Synons cannot destroy one another!"

Disregarding Tork's orders, Annilu's voice boomed from the larger dragon, puffs of flame billowing from the gaping mouth. "No. But are you willing to test whether The Living World can control your essence?"

Bandela summoned his most commanding voice. "Abominations! You threaten the very existence of this universe and the planet with which it is interdependent!" Lost on him was the irony of how similar those words were to those issued by TuMa'Aye Gra'Vay and her companion Synons when he had tried the same voice on them over a year before.

"Oh please." Rolling her eyes sarcastically, Marie Antoinette fluttered the painted fan she held. "Such melodrama."

The structure around them oscillated, shuddered, and collapsed into a chaotic mass of sparking energy.

"Did you do that?" Louis demanded.

"Of course not," Bandela replied. "Look beyond." His huge head swiveled to one side as a tremendous wing lifted to point in the same direction. What had previously been a radiant expanse of colorful energy emitting soothing vibrations was now thin, irregular threads of barely visible power hanging in a black void. "That's what left of the Realm."

Some of the revelers had banded together to direct their power toward repurposing the sparking Versailles remains into some semblance of the former Realm. Annilu was startled to sense regret and shame emanating from the former revelers. How could that be? Synons did not experience emotions in the manner of biological Earth creatures. How was it that she could perceive and identify these distinct emotions? What was happening?

"We appear to be evolving," the voice of Tu Ma'Aye Gra'Vay whispered in her mind. "You, like so many of us, resisted affinity with human feelings, although we've always linked with those of other Earth animals. Despite that, you began to absorb the essence of what makes them the unique beings they are. So did these and other Synons who spent time among them."

Annilu recalled her reactions while on Earth. "Now I'm aware of a sensation of shame," she admitted. "I emulated negative behavior characterizing resentment, scorn, even envy."

"It just proves you achieved some success in portraying a person. All of us who live closely with them reflect some of their positive and negative traits. If we can see it in ourselves—and learn to reshape it more positively—we can learn better ways of helping them. It's progress. I'm pleased with you, Annilu."

Annilu drifted toward those laboring to reshape the energy that represented their own worst behavior, joining their effort. She sent them kind words influenced by those she had just received.

Annilu felt the enveloping presence of Bandela and his two guards. The energy transformation quickened; chaotic sparks were reverting to the familiar radiance and harmonic vibrations of the Realm.

■　　■　　■

The decision to send Bandela to the Realm ended the island prison plan that had become fraught with problems. That left the issue of Bret, who was still imprisoned.

Mac visited Bret, finding a contrite being expressing profound regret. "We were sincerely affected by witnessing Earth's distress first hand. Not only Bandela and I, but the gang as well. It sort of brought us to our senses. We don't survive if she doesn't.

I'm pledging to work toward bringing all the renegades back into the fold. I'll start with my old gang who look up to me as a leader. Then I can dispatch them to convince others that their future is endangered by the actions of the very people they emulate. We can be very persuasive by appealing to the true Synon nature within us all. Please give me a chance to prove that I've reformed."

Bret sat patiently while Mac pondered. "You must understand that I don't trust you. No one can be spared to monitor you. The renegades must be reined in, of course. My inclination is to send you to the Realm; Bandela is proving true to his word there; he's disciplined its renegades. They still need more strong Synons like you. Perhaps, if you both demonstrate that you are trustworthy, you can return here in the near future to work with the Earth renegades."

Bret was visibly disappointed but nodded. "I understand your position. I'd probably make the same decision. Thank you for at least releasing me from prison."

"I'll arrange your transfer immediately. Good luck."

■　　■　　■

As human attitudes slowly evolved to reflect a renewed understanding of the many interlocking systems that kept Earth functioning, and the conditions optimal for life, positive energy flowed through the Passageways to the Realm, gradually rebuilding it. There was a long way to go, but if people didn't backtrack, conditions of life on both the Earth and in the Realm would continue to improve.

CHAPTER THIRTY

As the new North American Confluence center took shape, Judilay returned to assume temporary control until he could train a human telepath to take over.

On the flight, Judilay fell into deep contemplation. He was encouraged by Mac's confidence in his interpersonal and management abilities. Yet, he had allowed his desire to interact with people to mask his actual Synon mission by becoming immersed in humanity's emotional aspect, allowing Lana to form an inviable attachment to his persona. Judilay was confused by his own reactions. Tami had intimated that Synons might be evolving to better influence human behavior through understanding how their emotions drove it. Perhaps she was right; if so, there were boundaries that had to be rebuilt through honest dialogue among themselves and the people they lived among.

When Judilay was reunited with Lana, he felt her strong response. He experienced the same sensations that had at first elated him but were now a source of concern for her well-being. When they had the opportunity to be alone he would address it.

■　　■　　■

Lana struggled not to overwhelm Judilay with her feelings. She had never felt the intensity of intimacy as that shared within her and Judilay's psychic link. Perhaps it was simply the novelty and newness of the experience. She hoped that was the case.

After his welcoming reception they were able to walk together privately. Lana sensed a conflict within Judilay and asked what was bothering him.

He turned to her. "Lana, Synons are obviously evolving. We don't know where it will lead. Our mission is to continuously nourish and maintain humanity's link to the Realm through their connection with each other and Nature. To accomplish that, we've lived among you in deception, allowing you to see us as flesh and blood people with human emotions. We aren't. We're balls of energy. We play at being human. I'm sorry if my choice of persona and eagerness to interact like a person triggered a natural human response in you that can't be fulfilled. I can't be what you deserve. We share ideas, convictions, and so much more. What I can be is a steadfast friend."

Tears filled Lana's eyes. "I know," she whispered. "Intellectually, I understand everything. It's true, I've become infatuated with your persona. I simply must redirect my feelings. It's a gift to be able to share thoughts with you. We do, and will continue to, have a uniquely rewarding friendship that will enable us to help each of our own peoples moving forward." She couldn't bring herself to use the word "species."

Lana continued, forestalling his reply. "Our experience is one that will affect human telepaths as well when they interact. We must address it in our training and counseling. Right now, I'm just happy to have you here as a friend."

"We've been thinking too narrowly," Tami said. She had thought it important to leave the Realm and appear "in person" at yet another urgent meeting of the core people and Synons of the Earth Project. Jeff had called it to convey what Earth had just embedded in his mind—"they," who were the only ones who could help her, were all of humanity, not just telepaths.

Lew responded, "We all fell victim to the assumption that only someone special can solve great problems. It's intrinsic in human mythology. Perhaps we Synons see ourselves as those special ones, setting ourselves above humans because of our attributes."

Mac was characteristically brusque. "Our task is to redirect our plan, not to reflect on the past."

Jeff's hand raked his hair. "For what it's worth, I think Confluence members have already implemented the necessary action. They've engaged the whole world in information-sharing, dialogue, and action. It was done spontaneously, not by a direct plan to enlist certain people. They set out to incorporate everybody."

Emma pouted. "We would've done that if we'd known to." She brightened. "But now we kids can concentrate on making sure Earth is okay."

Lana spoke up. "I know you'll take good care of her." Then she addressed the group, "A lot of different people and organizations had already been trying to get everybody to see what has to be done, but they couldn't seem to reach those who really need to hear what they're saying."

Mac blustered. "Please focus on what actions we must take right now!"

Not intimidated by Mac, Mannie interrupted, "I think Lana was about to say that Jeff indirectly initiated this current global unity when he transmitted that image. It brought together tele-paths with the convictions and skills to build a worldwide initia-tive focused on saving Earth."

Marie spoke up, "Perhaps the original understanding of Earth's message wasn't wrong. It seems to have taken the emer-gence of Confluence to get this movement united and ready to do what's necessary on the planetary scale required."

Mac's mouth twitched with a smile. "I suppose I'll never get the hang of how people use rambling threads of thought to reach wise conclusions."

Jeff grinned. "Aw, Mac, you just need more time among us."

Suki addressed Jeff. "Are you perhaps ready to make some personal appearances?"

Sitting next to her, Cal remarked, "With the team Mac gave me as new Security Chief, I'll make sure you're safe every second." Although saddened by the loss of life, Cal had been relieved when the island plan had to be dropped. He was overjoyed to stay there with Suki in the mountains he had come to love.

Grinning, Chris said, "He's right. I'm coming on as his cyber guy. My new clearance gave me the chance to pump the right people for information on the latest gadgets and tactics."

Suki looked at Jeff. "Well?"

Jeff smirked. "I suppose I'm ready to talk in person. Can we start small?"

Lew's eyes twinkled. "It just so happens that I've been approached by some people who are very proud of Jeff and have invited him to speak among them. Just the place."

Jeff looked at him inquisitively. Marie sat with elbows on the table, hands in front of her smiling mouth. She had been con-sulted about the invitation.

Jeff looked around warmly at his family of friends. Within a couple of remarkable years his life had completely changed. He had confronted personal challenges and peril to Earth and beyond. With these people and Synons, along with a growing body of others, a better future could be forged for all. One area of regret lurked in his mind. When things quieted down enough he would address it. Little did he know Lew had just presented that opportunity.

*　　*　　*

The late autumn brought a delayed burst of color to the mountains. Accentuated by evergreens, the vivid reds, golds, and yellows of maples, oaks, dogwood, birch, and other deciduous tree species turned the landscape into a glorious canvas.

Among Nature's splendor, Jeff stood on the ground level stage of an Amphitheatre in Cherokee. Before him, sloping stadium seating was filled with friends, family, and extended family—his Native American brethren. Relaxed, he felt all nervousness vanish. He ignored the cameras and reporters.

Jeff sent his thoughts downward. There was no hint of the erratic wobble in Earth's rotation. A sense of contentment flowed into him.

He raised his arms and the crowd hushed. Jeff expressed his gratitude to everyone there and around the world who was joining to champion planet Earth.

"All living things are part of interconnected ecosystems that sustain us. Small imbalances can have widespread consequences, leading to cascading loss of habitat, resources, and life. Each time a species becomes extinct, it affects multiple others, including us.

"In the last few centuries, the actions of one species has increased the rate and intensity of warming. This has never before happened. In past times, the Earth warmed more slowly from natural processes. We have filled our atmosphere with greenhouse gases through the burning of fossil fuels. As a result, rapidly warming temperatures are melting glaciers and the polar icecaps, raising ocean levels that will soon threaten our coastlines and port cities. Rising ocean temperatures are destroying marine life, including the reefs that protect our coastlines from storm damage and flooding. We're all witnessing the climate extremes that are becoming the norm, characterized by more and stronger storms, wildfires, and droughts. Indeed, freshwater shortage is becoming chronic in many locations.

"Science tells us it's amazing that our species ever evolved. After roughly four billion years, we are a recent addition. Human civilizations date back only about five to six thousand years, if we define it as people living together in one place where they produce their own food and goods. It was a great leap forward for us to begin cooperating, building communities and cities, trading, and developing all that we see as a cooperative human society. We've steadily improved our standard of living and held fast to our core ethics and positive beliefs. However, we know there is a dark side, driven by the persistence of 'us-against-them' mindsets, individual greed, and thirst for power. We also like comfort and convenience, which we don't have to relinquish to save our planet. We just need to begin making changes in the way we do things.

"We already know ways to continue improving our lives, while also protecting the Earth and the life she sustains. Without them, without all the systems that the Earth maintains, our lives will steadily worsen until we can no longer exist. We need to keep searching for new and better ways to nourish the Earth the way she nourishes us. She can't do it without our cooperation.

"Our task is to help everyone understand one simple fact: we're all in this together. We are blessed with one planet on which we can continue to thrive if we act now."

Jeff felt a sense of belonging that he had never experienced. He was one with his people, the Earth and The Living World.

*   *   *

AFTERWORD

I am gratified by the support of those who read **Passageways: Book One** and **Precarious: Book Two** of **The Living World series.**

To best convey the theme, **Confluence** veers into fantasy while retaining science fiction elements. Since the book is at its core about Earth, the reader should perceive Earth's viewpoint along with that of other characters. In contrast to ancient and some contemporary cultures, we have come to see our species as separate from the planet we inhabit, rather than as an integral part of a planetary life system; I hope that personifying Earth sheds light on our interdependence.

Like the first two volumes, this book is set primarily in North Carolina, especially my beloved mountains. To touch on the global nature of the story, I've included settings and narratives set around the world. As in my prior books, I've taken some "poetic liberty" by inventing locations or mentioning actual ones. I enjoyed and learned much from the research necessary to portray these settings as accurately as possible. My apologies for any unintended misinformation or misconceptions in portraying these, as well as Native American culture. In exploring Jeff Hawke's connections to his Native American roots in Cherokee, North Carolina, I've included some references to that city and Cherokee culture. I'm proud of the Native American presence in my home state and want to highlight its value.

My thanks to Michelle Owen of Project Design, Inc., for taking a manuscript and turning it into files for a beautiful book. On our cover, Michelle selected another thematic detail from the same stunning image of The Carina Nebula NGC3372 as Books One and Two. This assemblage of 48 frames was taken by the Hubble Space Telescope. Please see the Copyright page for its full credit.

Please follow me on:

My Amazon Author page: **https://www.amazon.com/author/ patriciavestal-livingworld-bks**

My Facebook Author Page where you can comment and ask questions: **https://www.facebook.com/pvestalauthor**

For my blog and more information on ordering my books, visit **www.seaofmountainspress.com**

I appreciate and learn from reviews posted on the sites where you purchase my books. If you prefer to have your favorite bookstore order for you, they can do so through Ingram.

Again, thanks to all who read this series. It is written as entertaining speculative fiction, but I hope it prompts everyone who reads it to a renewed appreciation of Nature and to do whatever seems appropriate and feasible to help our unique Earth and the life it sustains to continue to be healthy.

ABOUT THE AUTHOR

Patricia Vestal is the author of ***Passageways: The Living World Book One*** and ***Precarious: The Living World Book Two***. After working in publishing and higher education in New York, and Florida, Patricia Vestal has returned to her native North Carolina's mountains that appear in her novels. Patricia's other publications include short fiction, reviews, and essays. Her plays have had readings and stage and television productions. She's a member of the North Carolina Writers Network, the Dramatists Guild, and the Alliance of Independent Authors. She earned her Communications BA from State University of New York and an MA in Drama from New York University.

Follow her at **www.seaofmountainspress.com** and **https://www.facebook.com/pvestalauthor.**

ABOUT CONFLUENCE

This stirring Solarpunk conclusion to **The Living World** trilogy immerses the reader in a world in which climate and geological apocalypse looms, while humanity is preoccupied with entrenched ideas and behavior that exacerbate the crisis. Coaxed by the self-serving rogue Bandela, Synons in the Realm and on Earth have strayed from their mission to strengthen humanity's diminishing link to Nature—a link that sustains the Realm. That energy-mind-spirit based universe is on the verge of vanishing.

In North Carolina's mountains, as Jeff Hawke trains young telepathic Uniques, his abilities propel him beyond the others in ways that change his life. Jeff is thrust into personal challenges and called upon to lead efforts against existential peril to Earth and beyond.

Extraordinary experiences occur, impelling Synons and Uniques to raise the possibility that they were initiated by The Living World, while ordinary people share unconfirmed rumors about recent unexplained events. Amid rising conflict, the movement to save Earth struggles to gain momentum. Can the future of Earth and the life she sustains be secured before it's too late?